Always gripping. Always new.

This is what NEW DESTINIES is all about . . .

. . . Carmen Miranda's ghost, haunting Space Station Three—with Anne McCaffrey (and no dragons).

. . . jet jocks vs. g force: and the winner is—the ghost in the machine . . . Dafydd ab Hugh's "Those Greyout Blues."

. . . Cold Fusion, The Dark Side of the Force revealed: "Roachstompers" by S. M. Stirling.

. . . getting a grip on star travel: "Fly Me to the Stars" by Charles Sheffield.

Not enough? Then, Let's Kill NASA—Again—with James Hogan!

This and every issue of
New Destinies
is dedicated to the memory of
Robert A. Heinlein

Fall 1989

EDITOR IN CHIEF
Jim Baen

ASSISTANT EDITOR
Toni Weisskopf

MANAGING EDITOR
Kathy Hurley

EDITED BY
JIM BAEN

NEW DESTINIES

The Paperback Magazine
Volume VIII/Fall 1989

BAEN BOOKS

NEW DESTINIES, VOLUME VIII

Copyright © 1989 by Baen Publishing Enterprises

A Baen Books Original

Baen Publishing Enterprises
260 Fifth Avenue
New York, N.Y. 10001

ISBN: 0-671-69839-7

Cover art by Dennis Beauvais

First printing, September 1989

Distributed by
SIMON & SCHUSTER
1230 Avenue of the Americas
New York, N.Y. 10020

Printed in the United States of America

CONTENTS

Introduction

Those of you who follow New Destinies *will recall my editorial of last year, "Let's Kill NASA Today." In it I argued for trading in the Space Agency's funding for a tax credit for space-based investments. The basis of my argument was that NASA was a failure. Herein James Hogan argues that the negative consequences of NASA's failures are as nothing compared to those of its one big success . . .*

PAINT YOUR BOOSTER:
Apollo—What Might Have Been

James P. Hogan

It's difficult to believe, but twenty years have gone by since that July 1969 when the first footprint marked the surface of the Moon—twenty years since the heady days of a decade when America took up a political challenge on behalf of its President.

The space program was—or at least was perceived to be—the measure in the world's eyes of the worth of the American dream; a demonstration of its continuing fitness to defend and lead the non-Communist world, symbolizing America's standing in the Cold War. And, as in any war, once the goal of victory had been set the only thing that mattered was achieving it. Other considerations were swept aside and cost was no object.

The war was won. There were triumphant and ecstatic victory celebrations. The world applauded. In the heyday of it all, immediately after the Apollo 11 success, a Special Task Group created by Richard Nixon to chart

NASA's future options came up with three alternative scenarios. First was a three-pronged program consisting of a fifty-man Earth-orbiting space station, a manned lunar base, and a Mars expedition by 1985. This program would have required as mere incidentals the development of both a reusable shuttle to service the space station, and a deep-space tug to supply the lunar base. Second, a less grandiose scheme called for just the space station and its shuttle, with no lunar program and a delayed Mars mission. And third—the bleakest that seemed possible to contemplate in the light of the reception accorded the lunar landing—just the space station and shuttle, with no Mars mission at all. But it was to be a huge shuttle, with a fully reusable booster powered by air-breathing jet engines as well as heavy-lift rockets, and an orbiter the size of a 727 airliner.

Heady days, indeed.

What actually happened is now history. The mood of the country had changed. America, having placed and won its bet, cashed in its chips, lost further interest, and went home. The proposals were ripped from coast to coast, and NASA's budget was so severely slashed that three of the remaining Apollo missions had to be scrapped. Eventually only the shuttle remained of all the things that had been dreamed of—and a severely cut-down version of it at that, probably saved only by a hastily contrived deal with the Air Force. The money for Skylab and the Apollo-Soyuz project was granted, but grudgingly, and then only because both would use left-over Apollo hardware. In the next five years NASA's staff declined by twenty-five percent.

A spectacular crash, of truly Wall Street 1929 proportions.

Since a term from economics seems appropriate to describe this sudden change of fortune, let's digress for a moment to talk about economics, and in particular about the phenomenon of the "crash," or "depression," and the things that bring it about. Maybe the similarity runs deeper than mere analogy.

There is a widely held notion that depressions are a part of a boom-bust business cycle which comes inevitably as part of the price one pays for a capitalist economy. I shall contend, however, that this is a Marxist propaganda myth embraced by belief systems that don't, or don't want to, understand how economics works.

In a free-market economy, where prices are set by supply and demand, interest rates provide a natural and effective indicator of the investment climate and function as a stabilizer of the general economy. Interest is simply a special name for a particular kind of price: the going rate for renting out surplus capital. It follows the same laws as any other price and, if allowed to find its own level, transmits information and exercises a stabilizing influence by adjusting the supply available from those competing to lend out capital to the demand of those wishing to borrow.

This isn't to say that economic life doesn't have its ups and downs, of course. But in the overall picture, ups are never occurring everywhere at the same time, and neither are downs. While some industries are in decline, letting people go and able to pay only marginal rates, others are expanding and competing for capital and labor, bidding up wage rates and paying higher prices to obtain the skills and resources that they need. Some entrepreneurs, through greater experience or intelligence, pure luck, or for whatever other reason, will make the right decisions while others lose, and in the long run the marketplace will tend to select the better players. The overall scene across the economic ocean is one of choppy waters, with the waves that fall in one place providing the momentum for others to rise elsewhere; and the average level remains unaffected.

Such localized fluctuations are normal features of the business scene. They are not to be confused with the *general* depression: the across-the-board slump that sets in when it turns out that the entire business community has made wrong decisions all at the same time. When the whole ocean goes down at once, it means that someone, somewhere, has pulled the plug.

This is true, also, when an economy collapses everywhere at once. Like a naturally evolving, complex ecology—which it is—a freely interacting market is a superposition of millions of ongoing processes, feedback loops, compensating systems, and error-correcting mechanisms. The tests of survivability are harsh but effective. Inappropriate mutations soon die out, while sound ones flourish; changes that cause a decline of some species spell opportunities for others; every extinction opens up a niche for an alternative experiment. The result is a system that is rugged, inherently self-stabilizing, and highly resilient against catastrophic disruption from internal causes. Only external factors imposed upon the system as a whole can affect everything, everywhere adversely.

The same is true when the whole of the business community makes wrong decisions at the same time. Something external to it has sent it to the wrong signals. And the only power that commands a force capable of misdirecting the entire economic system of a nation—is government.

In other words, what brings about *general* economic depressions is not some inexorcisable demon residing deep in the the workings of the market system, but, on the contrary, intervention in those workings by governments, which are the only institutions that possess the force necessary to do so. And the more massive the scale of the intervention, the more severe the depression will be when it comes.

The implications regarding Apollo begin to take on a new significance in this light.

The way that governments create depressions is by first initiating inflationary booms, through the control they've acquired over the money supply. Such booms turn out to be temporary and are characterized by easy money and the illusion of prosperity that comes with inflationary growth. It's the kind of quick-fix that gets you votes today and puts off the reckoning until after you're home and dry.

The ability to print money out of thin air dilutes the value of dollars everywhere, thus reducing the real burden of government debt at the expense of other people's assets. It is, in effect, an invisible form of taxation, a sleight of hand whereby wealth disappears from other places and rematerializes in the state's coffers with no transaction at all having taken place.

Another way of avoiding political unpopularity by creating illusory prosperity is to expand credit, which has the same effects as increasing the money supply. Banks are licensed to write promisory notes to pay on demand more than has been deposited with them. The jargon for this practice is "fractional reserve banking," which sounds very technical and respectable. But if the rest of us do the same, by writing a bad check on the amounts *we* have on deposit, it's called fraud.

Such artificially created excesses of money and credit send the same signals to the investment community as real capital accumulated through earnings and savings, the result of which is to encourage "malinvestment" of capital, labor, and other resources into providing needs for which no real demand exists. But eventually malinvestments must liquidate. The prescription of continual credit expansion to postpone the reckoning has to be curtailed before it leads to hyper-inflation, and that's when the "bust" half of the cycle sets in. Wasteful projects are abandoned or scaled down to be salvaged as best they can; inefficient enterprises die; prices fall, especially those of capital goods relative to consumer prices; and interest rates rise.

The bust is a natural period of adjustment following the malinvestment resulting from the manipulations that created the boom. Both the boom and the bust are not features of the free-market system at all, but the results of interfering with it.

Probably the best thing that government could do to help once it has created a post-inflationary depression is to stay out of it and let the market recover in its own way. In actuality, however, the inevitable response is to apply remedies that are seemingly purpose-designed to make things worse and not better—which was what turned the 1929 depression into a decade-long slump.

When the bust hits, demands go up from every side for the government to "do something," and a further round of intervention follows to put right what the previous round put wrong. And so the pattern for the future is set. As the patient gets sicker with every spoonful of medicine, the only response that the doctors can conceive is to increase the dose. The underlying premise that the treatment is in fact a cure and not the poison is never questioned.

No one would doubt—would they?—that John F. Kennedy's announcement, on May 25, 1961, of the lunar-landing goal was first and foremost a *politically* motivated decision. Since Sputnik 1 in 1957 the Soviets had sent the first probe around the moon, obtained the first views of the lunar farside, launched the first Venus probe, orbited the first animal, and finally the first man, Gagarin, a month before Kennedy's announcement. American prestige needed a big boost, and the experts had advised that the big boosters the Soviets already had would be sufficient to gain them every significant "first" this side of a manned lunar landing. I'm not suggesting that the whole Apollo concept was dreamed up in a month as some commentators seem to imagine. What Kennedy approved were existing plans, which NASA had drawn up a full two years before. But NASA was a new administration, anxious to attract funds and with prestige goals of its own to pursue. In other words, its own motives were in turn political.

Hence, the American space industry became a political instrument, its business the nation's earner of political prestige. Other goals were subordinate, constituting intervention on a massive scale into the more natural evolutionary path that the postwar development of aerospace technology would otherwise have followed.

I'm not saying that government has no place in the space program. Defense is a legitimate function of government—in an ideal world we wouldn't need it, maybe, but this is the real one, and we do—and clearly the fulfillment of that function in the modern world requires an active role in space. Traditionally, the U.S. Government has aided research into selected areas of scientific endeavor—for example through the setting up of NASA's predecessor, NACA, in 1915, which produced excellent returns for the aviation industry for a modest outlay.

But to direct virtually the whole of the nation's aerospace resources and effort, to channel all of its outwardly-directed energies and thinking for a whole decide into a single, politically inspired goal? . . . This goes beyond healthy involvement and becomes total domination, which if it sets in for long enough, carries the danger of stifling dissent and institutionalizing conformity to the point where nobody can conceive any other way of doing things.

The way to get a wagon train safely through the mountains is to send dozens of scouts ahead in all directions. There might only be a single pass, but one of the scouts will find it and bring back the news. This is the kind of multiple approach that produces the inherent ruggedness of natural evolutionary systems and free-market economies. But when the wagon master, a council of elders, or a fire-and-brimstone preacher, acting on a hunch, signs written in the stars, faith in the Lord, or whatever, decrees which direction shall be taken, without any scouts being sent out, it's almost certain to be a wrong one.

This is the danger with malinvestments, too. The boom that Apollo ushered in was evident: the ready money, unlimited credit, and instant prosperity. . . . And subsequently we saw the inevitable depression, when the malinvestment—eventually, as it had to—liquidated.

Don't get me wrong. I'm not trying to belittle the technical and human achievements of Apollo, which were magnificent. But the truth was that, political prestige aside, nobody really needed it. The military had been making farfetched noises about national security needing a lunar outpost, but that was to attract attention and funds. Their true interests lay in long-range missiles, transatmospheric flight, and orbital observation. The foreseeable commercial potential at that stage was in communications, navigation, and earth-observation, again involving near-space. And despite the hype, the real scientific information bonanzas of the sixties and seventies as far as space was concerned came from unmanned probes like Viking, Mariner, and Voyager for a tiny fraction of the costs of the manned-flight program. As Arthur Clarke has suggested, the whole thing happened thirty years too soon.

What alternative pattern might we have been unfolding, then, if Apollo hadn't happened when it did, and in the way that it did?

In the fifteen years that had elapsed since the end of World War II, thinking and developments in advanced aerospace technology had been proceeding briskly but smoothly with the kind of divergence that characterizes a healthy evolutionary process. True, the U.S. had lagged in its development of big boosters, mainly because of the Air Force's commitment to preserving its fleets of manned bombers as the core of the policy of deterrence, which relegated ICBMs to second priority. The Soviets, with no viable long-range bomber force to worry about, had no such concern and forged ahead. It was *this one fact* that gave them their string of space firsts from Sputnik I through to the Gagarin flight.

But by 1955, the U.S. had a number of missiles under development with the potential for orbiting a satellite: there were the Air Force's Atlas, Thor, and Titan, the Army's Jupiter and Redstone, and the Navy's Polaris. It has been persuasively argued that von Braun's Army team at Huntsville could have put a payload in orbit by the end of 1955 using the Redstone—if it hadn't been for inter-service infighting and bureaucratic tangles—almost two years ahead of Sputnik.

As things were, by 1958 the Air Force was pushing for what seemed a natural extension of the series of rocket-plane flights that had culminated in the X-15 and built up a reservoir of accumulated experience and the team of crack pilots at Edwards AFB in California. The Air Force plans envisaged a successor designated the X-15B, which would have taken off like a rocket, gone into orbit, and landed like an airplane, carrying a crew of two—a strangely familiar pattern, now being resurrected many years later. Another, more ambitious, project was the MOL (Manned Orbiting Laboratory), again with a two-man crew, proposed initially for spy missions and man-in-space research. And further, with a target date tentatively set as the late sixties, there was the "Dyna-soar," a rocket-launched flying machine—as opposed to a ballistic capsule—that would operate up to 400,000 feet at twenty-one times the speed of sound— the kind of thing only now being talked about again in the form of the space plane. And NASA, formed in 1958 to promote civilian development of space, would initially have pioneered the kinds of unmanned scientific missions that turned out to be so productive.

We can only speculate about what might have followed if plans such as these had been realized, instead of sacrificed to the moon god, and their progeny permitted to be born. Once the MOL was up, it's a safe bet that the Air Force would find reasons for needing more of them. The Navy would want one because the Air Force has got one, and NASA would eventually want one too, because the Air Force won't allow civilians inside the MOL. Then the Air Force will want a bigger one because the MOL is small and obsolete and the Soviets are reported to be working on a better one.

If the Air Force had been allowed to mount its own manned program, it wouldn't have needed the shuttle, and NASA could have gone with the ESA-*Hermes*-like craft that it ended up proposing before politics made it grow again. And the major contractors, undistracted by constantly elbowing for places at a bottomless public trough, would probably be thinking along lines that would lead to TAV-like commercial transports, across-the-Pacific-in-two-hours and the turnaround time of a 747, once more sounding very much like things we're only beginning to hear talked about again today.

The picture this suggests is one of vigorous activity in near-Earth space, centered around a variety of orbiting stations and the vessels to supply them, extending through into the seventies and providing a natural jumping-off point for the moon and beyond. If the Soviets want to respond by bankrupting Siberia to send a hare with a Red Star there first, well, let them. The Western tortoise will overhaul it soon enough, as soon as the time is right. Since there is no Holy Grail to focus effort and channel imagination, the conceivers and designers of different projects are free to pursue different solutions to their varying needs, resulting in a proliferation of vehicles large and small, manned and unmanned, reusable and expendable.

Such a pattern would have continued the curve of improving performance for aerospace vehicles that had been climbing fairly smoothly since the beginning of the century, instead of introducing a huge discontinuity that only a massive, forcibly public-funded venture could hope to bridge, effectively locking the private sector out. I don't mean the giant contractors, whose interests lie as much at the political end of the spectrum as those of the Pentagon, or the major bureaucracy that NASA became, but the independent enterpreneurs whose image is traditionally synonymous with American enterprise. By the end of the fifties, with the rough ground having been broken by the bulldozers of postwar defense-funded ventures, perhaps the time was about right for a new wave of Rockefellers and Vanderbilts to organize and apply the kind of talent and ingenuity that brought the price of a barrel of oil down from four dollars to thirty-five cents, produced the Model-T Ford, and in more recent times the home computer. But in the climate of massive diversion of the industry's supporting infrastructure and the cream of its expertise into a thirty-billion-dollar, single-purpose spectacular, such possibilities were literally unable to get off the ground.

There were some private ventures despite all the obstacles, such as SSI of Houston who launched the *Conestoga* rocket, Starstruck Inc. with its *Dolphin*, and PALS with the *Phoenix*, and more recently Amroc with its hybrid rocket motor. But such initiatives were systematically frustrated by NASA pricing practices that took advantage of forced public subsidy and effectively wrote off development overheads.

Another obstacle to private development has been a reluctance of investors to put up front-money in the face of skeptical expert reactions to such concepts as MMI's "Space Van" which, it is claimed, will orbit payloads for six hundred dollars per pound instead of the tens of thousands of dollars that have come to be regarded as normal. But let's remember that the only experts available for would-be investors to seek advice from have all gained their experience and their world-view within the confines of the same elephantine bureaucracy, where the rewards come not for doing things simply and cheaply, but for managing the most prestigious departments and the biggest budgets. I worked for Honeywell in the sixties, when computers that cost hundreds of thousands of dollars—when money was money—and which lived in air-conditioned rooms were less powerful than ones we buy in supermarkets today for our children. The same experts who scoff at the idea of six-hundred-dollars-per-pound into orbit would also have laughed at the idea of an Apple, a Commodore, or an IBM PC.

In the computer business, perhaps the last remaining area of genuine free-market opportunity, we take dazzling leaps in performance and plummeting costs for granted. But when it comes to space, we have built acceptance of the inescapability of intractable complexity, gargantuan budgets, political entanglement, and mammoth project-management systems into our mindset of unconscious presumptions.

So much for the economic aspect of the post-Apollo depression. But at a deeper level there is a further irony that has to do with losing sight of the basic principles and values which the way of life that Apollo symbolized was supposed to stand for.

America was founded on the principles of liberalism— liberalism in the original sense of the word, before it became a victim of contemporary doublespeak—which asserted the sovereignty of the individual, recognized basic individual rights and freedoms, and relegated the task of the state to the purely passive function of protecting them. Under such a system anyone is entitled to own property and trade it freely; to think and say what he likes; and to live his life in his own way, to a degree consistent with the right of others to do the same, without its being forcibly subordinated to plans formulated for him by anyone else or by the state.

It's easy now, thirty years after the hysterical era of

McCarthy and the "missile gap," to see that Sputnik I did not signify a great overtaking of the Western way of life by the Soviet socialist utopia. Eisenhower saw it too and tried to downplay things to their proper proportions, but he miscalculated the reaction of the media, the public, and the world at large. It isn't really all that surprising that a totalitarian ruling elite, with the resources of a nation at their command, should be able to evoke an impressive performance in any single area of achievement that it selects as a demonstration. Building a pyramid is not so difficult when the haulers-of-blocks don't have any say in the matter.

Very well, so the Soviets got a big booster first—but even that needed a lot of help from squabbling generals and bungling bureaucrats on our side. America had developed the greatest production and consumer economy the world had ever seen, an agricultural system whose productivity was becoming an embarrassment, and an average standard of living exceeding that enjoyed by millionaires a hundred years previously, and more—all at the same time. The other guys were having to build walls and wire fences around the country to keep the inhabitants in the workers' paradises from flocking here.

Where the irony lies is that in seeking a tangible challenge to demonstrate the technological, scientific, and economic superiority of a free society, the planners turned to precisely the methods of centralized state-direction and control that their system was supposed to be superior to.

"We won. So our way is better," was the cry.

"Yes, but you had to use *our* way to do it!" was the retort that it invited.

The only debate was over *which way* the state should direct the program. The possibility that perhaps the state had its place, yes, but shouldn't be directing the overall form of the program at all was never entertained. As with the doctors arguing over the dose, the underlying premise that they were administering the right medicine was never questioned.

But the American economy was huge and robust. Even if Apollo was a long-term technological answer to a short-term political need, and even if it did represent something of a malinvestment, the effects could have been absorbed without undue damage. If we compare the cost with what the U.S. spends every year on such things as alcohol, cosmetics, or entertainments, it wasn't really so huge. The country could afford it. The crowning irony comes, perhaps, because its worst effect may have been due to the fact that it *succeeded*!

It's difficult to argue with success. Some of the history's worst disasters have been brought about by taking a solution that has worked successfully in one area and trying to apply it in another area where it isn't appropriate. And the greater its success in the past, the more persistently will its advocates try to apply it to new problems, long after it has become obvious that it isn't working.

An example is the stupendous success of the physical sciences in the centuries following the European Renaissance, when the new methods of reason brought insight and understanding to subjects that had been dominated by dogma and superstition for a thousand years. By the eighteenth century, apologists and enthusiasts for science saw scientific method as the panacea for all of humanity's problems. If science could unify astronomy and gravitation, heat and mechanics, optics and geometry, then surely science could accomplish anything. Poverty, injustice, inequality, oppression, and all of the other social problems that had plagued mankind since communal patterns of living first evolved, would all disappear in the scientifically planned, rational society.

Unfortunately (or is it?), people are less obliging and predictable than Newtonian particles, and tend to frustrate grand uptopian designs by having ideas of their own about how they want to live. A society of individuals who were free to dissent and choose would never yield the kind of consensus that the various schools of early French and German socialism required on how to decide priorities and allocate resources. Hence, the institutions of a free society become obstacles to the Plan and must be removed. And once the individual and his rights become subservient to the state's collectively imposed goals, society takes the first step down the slippery slope that leads towards the secret police, the Gestapo, the Gulag, and the concentration camp.

Apollo left a generation of administrators and legislators imbued with the conviction that if centralized government control and massive federal spending can land men on the Moon, then big government programs are the way to accomplish anything. Poverty, injustice, inequality, oppression, will all be cured by progressively larger doses of the same measures that have achieved just the opposite everywhere else they've been tried.

Yes, massive, state-directed programs can achieve results. They can produce big booster rockets, or build pyramids, or plant flags on the Moon with high PR coverage at a cost that no one would pay for freely—if that's what you want to do. But they don't solve social problems.

As I see it, the real problem was not so much the program itself—it represented a comparatively small proportion of the American GNP and was probably the kind of medicinal binge that the nation needed anyway—but the massive social programs inappropriately modeled on the rationale of Apollo, afterward. It's difficult to argue with success, however, even if the success is irrelevant, and when the promised results fail to materialize, inevitably the response is to increase the dose.

The spectacle of government directing the nation to the successful conquest of the Moon became the model. The original ideal of a people free to direct their own lives with government functioning in a passive, protective capacity faded, and politics has become an arena of contest for access to the machinery of state to be used as a battering ram for coercing others. The only debate is about *whose* views the state's power should be used to impose. The notion that it shouldn't impose *anyone's* is forgotten.

As space came to be seen by the majority as posing such immense problems that only government could hope to tackle them, so society has turned increasingly to government for direction in the everyday aspects of living that were once the individual's own affair: to insure his health and security, to guarantee him a livelihood, to educate his children, to protect him from his errors, to compensate him for the consequences of his own foolishness, and to tell him what to think.

Yes, we got there first. But who won the race?

What lessons would the younger generations today have learned from growing up with, working in, and absorbing the value system of an independent, self-reliant, free-thinking people—government in its proper capacity, business corporations, scientists, and crazy individualists—charting its own expansion into space in its own way, according to its own needs, for its own reasons? What the world never had a chance to see was a society free to evolve its own pattern of discovering, exploring, using, and adapting to the space environment.

For a true evolutionary pattern is just that: undirected. Only egocentric, Ptolemaic man could imagine that evolution was directed toward perfecting intelligence. Every eagle knows that it was directed toward perfecting flight, every elephant that it was to greater strength, and every shark that it was to perfecting swimmers.

But in reality, evolution isn't directed *toward* anything. Evolution proceeds *away from*. Away from crude beginnings and less desirable solutions, and on to better things that can lie in a thousand different directions. As the wagon-train song says, "Where am I going, I don't know. Where am I off to, I ain't certain. . . ."

But in that direction lies all that is truly new, exciting, revolutionary, and beyond the wildest dreams of even the most creative planners.

And *that*, maybe, would have shown the Soviets, and the world, something that was really worth knowing.

Introduction

I have been accused of using New Destinies as a showcase for material to be published in other Baen books, of favoring our own over other titles in an effort to promote them. Well, I am shocked—simply shocked— that anyone could think such a thing. It is pure coincidence that this story is the lead piece in the most Bizarre of all possible shared universes: Carmen Miranda's Ghost is Haunting Space Station Three.

IF MADAM
LIKES YOU . . .

Anne McCaffrey

"It's green for go, fellas," said the Systems Engineer, his bony face wreathed with a weary but satisfied expression. He leaned back in the chair, arching his spine until all heard a muted "crack."

Migonigal, the Portmaster, winced and grinned comically at his assistant, Sakerson, his shipmate, Ella Em and Rando Cleem who manned the suspect glitched mainframe.

"And?" Migonigal prompted.

"And what? You had a couple of sour chips, five worn circuits, a wonky board, and some faulty connections—according to my diagnostics. Nothing serious."

"Nothing serious! Nothing serious?" Migonigal echoed himself as he turned a stunned expression to the others.

"But what caused the . . ." Sakerson began but Migonigal cut him off with a sharp slice of his thick fist.

"Your basic system is jolly good," the SysEng said, rising and stretching his arms over his head. This time a crick in his neck went "pop." He patted the console affectionately. "Well designed. However I upgraded your Mainframe with a couple of new programs. An internal systems check so this won't happen again. You know how cost-conscious the Space Station services are," he went on as he packed up his service kit. "And I installed new holographics software to help you guys dock faster."

"Docking isn't a problem," Migonigal said, disgruntled, but he signed the others not to pursue the matter. "Look, need any fresh tucker from our hydro garden?" he asked ingratiatingly as the SysEng zipped himself into his space gear. "We've got some beaut . . ."

The SysEng gave a scornful snort. "I got better'n they issue you lot, and I don't have to share." He beckoned closer to Migonigal in a conspiratorial fashion. "The ghost I hear tell you guys got . . ." Migonigal leaned away from the man in denial. "Just a sour chip in the visualization program. You won't have trouble now."

"A sour chip?" Migonigal's bass voice travelled incredulously up an octave to end on a despairing note. Sakerson crossed his fingers behind his back and he noticed Rando making an odd warding gesture. Ella grunted her disgust with the SysEng.

"Hey, what's this?" The SysEng had picked up his helmet in which now reposed a yellow banana. "Hey, maybe you guys got something I haven't at that? Got any more where this came from?"

Migonigal stifled a groan and shrugged again, spreading his hands and grinning. "Could be. But I'm hoping that is the last one."

"Yeah, well, ta very." And, peeling the fruit, the SysEng bit off a hunk, chewing with pleasure. "Hey, just ripe too. Okay, I'm off. Check me out, will you, mate? I'm due at Wheel Four in two days. Gotta burn it!"

Migonigal signaled for Sakerson to escort the specialist to his vehicle, moored at Dock 4 which was nearest the control module.

"Anything we should know about the updates?" Sakerson asked as he followed the SysEng down the corridor, his felt slippers making no noise on the plasrub flooring.

"All I did was wipe the glitches and load the new programs. Same general format as the old . . ." A wicked grin over his shoulder at Sakerson, "And exorcised your ghoulies and ghosties." He chuckled his amusement.

"Fine. Thanks!" Sakerson could not keep the sarcasm out of his voice as he paused at the control module.

"Catch," the SysEng added, flipping the empty banana skin at Sakerson. "Biodegradable, you know! This station needs all it can get." The portal closed on his healthy guffaw, and with Sakerson bereft of any suitable rejoinder.

It had been ignominious enough to have had to call in a Systems Engineer to check the mainframe, in the unlikely case that . . . recent developments were a systems malfunction. While all the stationers had examined their . . . inexplicable problem among themselves at great length
    no one was bassakward enough to let a whisper of it off Three. Just like a SysEng to "know" it all before he'd even docked.

With a sigh, Assistant Portmaster Sakerson threw the skin at the nearest disposal hatch on his way back to the control center, wishing it was something else that apparently wasn't biodegradable.

When Sakerson reentered the control room, Ella was on Console, completing the debarkation routines. The SysEng's flashy little ftl drifted down-away from Space Station Three's Wheel before ignition and the flare vanished quickly in the twinkle of star blaze. Sakerson registered, and appreciated, the Portmaster's sour expression.

"Well?" Migonigal asked his spacemate.

"Well," Ella replied with a shrug, giving the console one more tap. "Program sure ran smooth. But *it* always did. I just can't see how *she* could materialize, or whatever she does, in a mainframe built a hundred years after she breathed her last. It doesn't compute. It also doesn't make any sense." She rose and gave the disconsolate Migonigal a hug and a kiss, winking over his shoulder at Sakerson. "Little enough to titillate folks stuck out in the Void. Been kinda fun to have *something* to puzzle out."

Migonigal gave her a wide-eyed look of dismay. "But if that wag-winged SysEng spreads this around . . ."

"You're a good Portmaster, sir, with a clean record," Sakerson said stoutly. "SS-Three's never had any effups, bleeds, crashes or leaks. It's a good station and a good crew. Besides, we can always say it's just a new game."

To relieve the boredom of off-duty, "leisure" hours, Space Stations, Wheels and Mining Platforms were immensely creative, given their limited recreational facilities. There was an ongoing informal competition to invent new "games," physical or mental. The good ones circulated.

"That's it, Sakersonboy, you tell him," Ella said, grinning. "He won't believe me and I've been his mate for yonks!" She glanced at the chrono. "Your watch, Sakersonboy. C'mon, Miggy, Rando says his new war starts at 2100, and I'm gonna whip that war-ace no matter how long it takes me."

In self-defense, and to keep from thinking about their—apparition and "her" habits—Rando Cleem had started a long drawn-out "war," winning battle after battle no matter who was his opponent.

"Us," Migonigal corrected her, letting himself be drawn out of the control room. "I figured out the tactics that had his forces retreating last watch . . ." The panel slid shut over the rest.

Sakerson grinned ruefully. He envied Migonigal for Ella. She was all that a fellow could want in a spacemate. Trouble was that, when Sakerson had been assigned to Space Station Three six months ago, everyone was paired off, one way or another, with the exception of Sigi Tang who was near retirement and Iko Mesmet who never left the spin-chambers. Sakerson tried not to feel like odd man out but his singleness was beginning to get to him.

He took the console seat for it was now time for the routine station status check. When Sakerson began to log the results in, he really did see an improvement in the speed at which the data was reported. Once the report was finished, Sakerson altered his password. SysEngs were supposed to be discreet but no one liked to think that even the most close-mouthed head in the galaxy had accessed personal data. There were fifty-nine minutes before any further routine, no scheduled arrivals, and his relief was not due for another two hours.

Rubbing his hands together, Sakerson ran a test check, to familiarize himself with the new internal systems check. That activity soon palled because, despite his proficiency and a half year's familiarity with SS-3's mainframe, he could discern the subtle minor alternations. He had his hand halfway to the switch to looksee what was happening to Rando's war in the staff leisure facility but he wasn't really that interested. Rando always won. He had reactions like the station's cat and must have been sleeping on military history & strategy tapes. Great man, Rando, even if he did see ghosts. Girl ghosts. Pretty girl ghosts. Cuddly girl ghosts! Sakerson hadn't seen a manifestation though he'd found a lot of cherries in his bunkspace. Rando had pronounced her vivaciously attractive which had annoyed his spacemate, Cliona, considerably.

Sakerson liked a calmer, dignified type of girl, but not as phlegmatic as Sinithia, the unflappable station medic. Tilda, who was Trev's mate, was aggressive and went in for Kwan doh with an enthusiasm only Rando matched. Trev usually watched. It didn't do, he'd told Sakerson privately, for two spacemates to get too physical with each other. (Having watched Tilda spar, Sakerson decided that she could deck Trev anytime she liked. It was shrewd of Trev to let her work steam off on Rando.) In any event, while there were some very good-looking female persons on board, not one had indicated they might prefer his company to that of their present attachment.

A green flashing light on the visual pad caught his attention. "SPECIFY." Sakerson blinked. He didn't remember turning on the holography program but the amber-lit pad was on.

"SPECIFY WHAT?"

"APPEARANCE."

Some had said that the Carmen Miranda ghost had been generated by the holography circuits. The SysEng had put paid to that theory. But Sakerson gulped because he hadn't, to his knowledge, accessed the pad.

Then he grinned. Well, he could check the new software out, and have a bit of fun. He'd program the girl of his dreams and see what came up. He wouldn't mind a ghost of his own creation. Preferably one that didn't leave bananas where a guy could slip on the mushy things.

He entered in the spirit of the exercise so completely that the bells of change of watch sounded before he had quite finished the holograph. He just had time to name the file "Chiquita," thinking of the SysEng's banana skin, before he filed it away under his new password. He grinned as Rando arrived, certain that would be one of the first things the war-ace would also do.

"Did you win, Rando?"

"No contest," Rando replied, slipping into the chair Sakerson vacated.

"How many does that make?"

"Hell, I lost count. Easily over the 1800 mark now."

Which was nearly as many as the Station's previous war-ace had achieved.

"Have a quiet one," Sakerson said in traditional exit fashion.

He had a light meal before going to his space, jetting himself clean before he netted down in his bunk. But sleep eluded him as his thoughts kept returning to the unfinished holograph. He had her a shade too short—he'd have to bend awkwardly to kiss her. Much more comfortable to just bend his head slightly. And the shape of her face should be oval, rather than round. He'd rather she had high cheek bones to give her face character, and a firmer jaw. The retrousse nose wouldn't fit the cheekbones: make it delicate and longer, and a broad higher brow. He'd got the hair just right, swinging in black waves to her shoulder blades. Sometimes she'd wear it up, the ends curling over the top of a head band. He'd seen some beautifully carved scrimshaws, plastic but stained and polished like old ivory. One would go great against black hair.

The eyes provided a quandary. He vacillated between a medium green and a brilliant light blue. Then he compromised. One would be the green, the other the blue. He'd had a station mate on Alpha-2 with a blue eye and a brown eye. She said it was a genetic trait.

He hovered between a cheek dimple or a cleft in the chin—he'd seen a very beautiful pre-Silicon Age actress who'd had a fetching cleft. His mind made another tangent—would a cinema search break the monotony of Rando winning wars? Or better still, song titles!

"I'm Chiquita Banana and I'm here to say . . ."

Unbidden, the advertising jingle popped into his head. Old Rando wouldn't do well in that kind of game, now would he? All he ever read were strategy treatises and he only watched ancient war movies. Of course, movie wars was all there were.

Having called up the silly tune, Sakerson found it hard to shake and ended up having to go through his Serenity Sequence to get to sleep.

"One thousand eight hundred and twelve wars is enough!" Trev yelled, enunciating carefully. "That is all, Rando, finito! The wars are over."

"Yeah, and what're we going to do now?"

" 'The skin you love to touch'," Sakerson said, grimacing ludicrously and smoothing the back of his left hand with his fingers, blinking his eyes coyly. " 'Eighteen hour one'."

Rando stared at Sakerson. "What's wrong with him?" Trev shrugged.

"What's the reference?" Sakerson asked, snapping a finger at Rando. "A new game—spot the product from the jingle!"

" 'The skin you love to touch'?" Rando guffawed. Then he paused, rolling his eyes. Rando was a competitor: he hated to lose—anything. "Okay, how much boning up time do we get?"

"Anytime you're off shift," Sakerson replied, feeling generous. The brief scrolling he'd done in the history of advertising reassured him. Not even Rando's rattrap mind could encompass all the variations of the centuries. Hell, most big companies changed slogans three and four times a year. The Madison Space Platform was named for the industry that started on the famous Ave-

nue, in honor of all the catch phrases that had generated enthusiasm for The Big Step. "Warm-up game
tomorrow 1300 in the wardroom."

By 1400 the next day, half the off-duty stationers
were there, nearly forty players, and Trev had programmed a tank to display the distinctive logos and
watchwords. Sakerson got a buzz watching the enthusiasm of the players. In another day, it had become a fad
to log in and out with some catchy slogan or whistled
tune. A lot of people spoke to Sakerson in the aisles and
corridors who had never noticed him before and he was
feeling pretty good with himself. Except that he still
occupied single space. He keenly felt a woman need
and there was simply no match for him on SS-3.

Out of this sense of lone-ness, he called up the
Chiquita program again and made the alterations he
had considered that first night. She was real pretty, his
Chiquita, dark curls falling from the head band, a trim
tall figure in her station togs. And he extended his
daydream beyond physical appearance.

Chiquita had a quick mind, and a temper. She was a
. . . medic? . . teacher? . . . programmer . . . engineer . . . quartermaster . . . Yeah, quartermaster would
fit in with his goal of Portmaster. Space required more
and more stations as way-points, beacons in the deep
Void, manned and ready to guide the merchantmen,
cargo drones, and passenger cruisers as well as providing "shore leave" space for naval personnel. A good
team complemented each other, like Migonigal and
Ella, Cliona and Rando, and Tilda and Trev. Chiquita
would have been asteroid-belt born, comfortable with
life on a space station because too often the planet-born
got to yearning for solid earth under their feet or wind
in their face or some such foolishness. She'd maybe
have done some solid-side time in university so she had
polish. A spacer should have experienced the alternative so s/he'd know what s/he wasn't missing. Sakerson
hadn't minded four years study on Alpha Ceti but he'd
been bloody damned glad to get posted to the Alpha-2
Platform, and on to Station Three . . . in spite of recent
"occurrences."

Then, too, the job was getting too much for the present Quartermaster, old Sigi. On the one hand, everyone did their best to help the old guy—hell, he was Original Personnel—but there came a time when you couldn't cover up because it endangered the Station.

Sakerson turned back to the more pleasant pastime. He tried to imagine Chiquita's laugh: some girls looked great and had laughs like . . . like squeezed plastic. And she'd have a real sparkle in her eyes so you had a clue to her inner feelings. And she'd have them, too. Straight dealing, straight talking so he wouldn't have to think up alternatives the way Trev did with his Tilda.

He heard someone beyond the panel and he fumbled across the keys to save Chiquita to his personal file before Migonigal entered to relieve him of duty.

"No problems?" the Portmaster asked him, looking at the main panel with raised eyebrows.

"None, sir. None at all. Quiet watch, all status reports logged in quiet, too," Sakerson replied, staring the Portmaster right in the eye to prove his innocence.

"Hmmm, well, thought I saw a send flash. Personal correspondence has to go out in the public spurts, Sakerson."

Sakerson now looked back at the terminal but the only color showing was the green of stability and order.

"I know that, sir. Have a quiet."

Migonigal flashed him a quick look. "Is that a slogan, too?"

"Up here, maybe," Sakerson replied with a grin.

He left without unseeming haste and gave the matter no further thought. Until it was sleeptime and he had to slow himself down after a rousing game of Slogan which he had won on points. Rando wasn't the fastest eidetic on board, not by a longshot. In fact, it soon began to take all Sakerson's free time to keep ahead of Rando on the history tapes to air more and more esoteric slogans and score Rando down.

" 'The world's finest bread?' "

"Silvercup!"

" 'Let them eat cake'!"

"Not an advertising slogan! Disqualify!"

" 'When it rains, it pours!' "

"What about 'never scratches'?"

" 'Good to the last drop'?"

" I'd walk a mile for a Camel.' "

"What's a camel???"

" 'Nestle's make the very best . . .' what?"

"Hey, does it have to be a product, Sakerson?"

"It has to be a slogan."

"Gotcha this time, then," Trev chortled. " 'Only YOU can prevent forest fires.' "

"Forest fires? That's prehistoric!"

"Yeah, but whose slogan was it?"

"I got one—'You'll wonder where the yellow went . . .' "

"No fair, you gotta give the whole slogan. Give us a break!"

" 'Call for Philip Morris!' "

"Who he?"

"You mean, what's he."

"Keep it clean, gang, keep it clean."

"That's not a slogan."

"No, good advice!"

Everyone caught the fever and the station sizzled as much as it had when the ghost rumor started. They sent the game on with the crew of the freighter *Marigold*, the light cruiser *Fermi* and the destroyer *Valhalla*. Space Station Four beamed for the rules and then Tilda had the bright idea of trading them with Mining Platform Tau Five for twenty cases of prime gin: a grand change from Cookie's raw rum. A passenger liner bought Slogan for three carcasses of authentic earth beef meat and the Mess voted Sakerson free drinks for a week. Which, since he didn't drink much anyhow, Sakerson thought was spurious, but he took it as being a gesture of good will.

Of course, Chiquita wouldn't mind a drink or two, and she'd be very good at Slogan: nearly as quick as he was.

" '99 and 44/100% pure—it floats.' "

"Let's not mess up the Station now, gang!"

" 'Damn the torpedoes!' "

"Not applicable!"

"Well, it became a warcry."

"Warcries are not slogans!"

"I don't see why not! A slogan's a slogan. It stands for something!"

"What does 'damn the torpedoes' stand for?"

"Not surrendering when faced with invincible odds!"

" 'Nuts to you!' " Rando shouted, finally getting a chance to play.

The Police Vehicle hailed Space Station Three while Sakerson was on duty and protocol required that the Portmaster be summoned for such official arrivals. The PV came from Alpha, priority mission, coded urgent.

"I dunno," the Portmaster said, scrubbing his short-cropped grey hair. "What's the priority, Captain?" he asked the PV.

"Urgent personnel orders, Portmaster Migonigal! Just let us nose in. I've got the requisition and travel papers. Shipshape and bristol fashion, highest priority. I'm putting them in the scan now. Hear you've got some good gin aboard for a change."

"Commencing docking procedures, Captain," Migonigal replied stiffly. "Sakerson, you have the conn. Dock this . . ."—the pause said 'sodding so-and-so'—"vehicle. I've got to tell Sigmund to hide some of the gin." The PV's had been known to drink a station dry: hospitality decreed that the defenders of the Void should have unlimited access to Station consumables. "He would know about the gin," the Portmaster said with a rueful sigh. "And what in hell is he bringing in? I don't remember requisitioning anything recently, certainly nothing high priority that requires police escort!"

"They might just have been first available space, sir," Sakerson said, busy with hands and eyes on the delicate task of matching the three dimensional speeds and shapes of a large Space Station and a very small, fast PV.

"Now, how the hell could this happen?" Migonigal demanded, watching the printout on the scanner. His question was not rhetorical but Sakerson could not spare a glance. "You can ask and ask and ask for something essential, even critical, and you can't get them to shift ass below and send it up. I could have sworn I hadn't forwarded Sigi's transfer to Control. And here I've got a replacement." Migonigal sounded totally mystified. "Not a bad looker, either." Migonigal snickered. "Makes a nice change from old Sigi. Time he retired anyhow."

"Ship's locked in, Portmaster," Sakerson said, leaning back with a sigh. Big ships were a lot easier to dock. He glanced over at Migonigal's screen and nearly fell out of his chair.

"Yeah, pretty as a picture," Migonigal went on, oblivious to the consternation of his assistant. "Perez y Jones, Chiquita Maria Luisa Caterina, b. 2088, Mining base 2047, educated Centauri, specialty, Quartermaster. Not that much experience but we only need someone who can remember to order what we need and where it's stored."

Sakerson stared with panic-widened eyes at the ID scan. This had to be the weirdest coincidence in the galaxy. Granted, that out of the trillions of physical possibilities, someone vaguely resembling his "dream" girl was theoretically possible, but the probability . . . Sakerson's mind momentarily refused to function. HOW? The mainframe had just been vetted: all the boards, the circuits; there hadn't been so much as a tangerine or a cherry appearing for a week, nothing since the SysEng's banana.

"I'll go down and greet her, give Sigi the good news. He won't believe it either. Yeah, while I'm doing courtesy, you call Sigi and tell him to save some of the gin for his farewell blast." Migonigal left Sakerson to stare at the visual realization of his imagined perfect woman.

After his watch, it took all Sakerson's courage to enter the wardroom. He could hear the laughter, the cheerful conversation always stimulated by the arrival of new personnel. Everyone would be getting to know her, getting to know HIS Chiquita! Rando might horn in, he and Cliona had had that brawl over slogans . . . Sakerson resolutely entered the cabin.

"You gotta avoid this guy, Chiquita," Rando exclaimed, seeing him first. "He's the weightless wit responsible for Slogan!"

As she turned to look at him, Sakerson's throat closed and he couldn't even gargle a greeting. She was *his* holo, from the slight cleft in her chin, to the way her hair was dressed, curling over a band, green eye/blue eye and sparkling, with a grin of real welcome on her sweetly curved lips. She held out a hand and even her nails were as he had imagined: long ovals, naturally pink. Dreamily, he shook her hand, reminding himself to release it when he heard a titter.

"I'm pleased to meet the man who invented Slogan," she said, her eyes sparkling candidly. How come he hadn't realized that her voice would be a clear alto?

He slid into the free chair and grinned, hoping it didn't look as foolish as it felt, plastered from ear to ear, because he couldn't speak, couldn't even stop grinning.

"Slogan's all you hear about Station Three these days," she went on, not dropping eye contact, although her left hand strayed briefly to her hair.

"That makes a nice change," Sakerson managed to say, making his grin rueful. He knew from the tilted smile on her lips and the sparkle in her eyes that she had heard the ghost rumor.

"Now," Rando said, breaking in, "War games are far more a test of intelligence and foresight."

"Oh, war games," she said, dismissing them with a wave of her hand and further entrancing Sakerson, "I played every war game there is when I was growing up on the MP. And won!" Deftly she depressed Rando's bid. "Now Slogan stimulates the brain cells, not adrenaline." She wasn't coy, she wasn't arch, but the way she looked sideways at him made Sakerson's heart leap. "Say, didn't you dock the PV?"

"I did."

"You're smooth!"

"Watch it, Chiquita," Rando warned. "This guy's dangerous. He's single-spaced."

Ignoring Rando's thinly-veiled leer, Chiquita tilted her head up to Sakerson and just smiled.

"Give over, lout," Cliona told her mate, elbowing him playfully out of the way. "Say, Chiquita, how'd you snaffle a posting like Three?"

Chiquita lifted both hands and shrugged. "I don't really know. I didn't think I was very high on the short list. And then suddenly I was handed orders, shoved towards the PV as the first available vehicle coming this way." She flashed a charming smile around the wardroom. "But it's great to be in such good space!"

"Why waste space?" Sakerson demanded, winking at her.

Even in the free and easy atmosphere of a space station, where personnel have little privacy and every new association is public knowledge, Sakerson did not rush Chiquita. She had indicated a preference for the way his mind worked and, more directly, that she liked his physical appearance. He let her get settled into the routine and waited until the next day before he asked her to the hydroponic garden. She smiled softly and winked at him before turning back to her supply texts. Like any space bred girl, she knew perfectly well what generally happened in such facilities.

"This is a splendid hydro," she said, and paused as the path took them to the banana palm. "Well now," and she flushed delicately so that Sakerson knew she was aware of the Slogan for her name, "How . . . how very unusual."

"That's tactful of you," Sakerson said before he realized that his words were tantamount to an admission of the truth of the scuttlebutt.

"I think you're tactful, too," she replied and stood right in front of him. It would have taken a much more restrained man than Sakerson to resist the urge to see if he only had to bend his head. So he did.

Then, just after they had thoroughly kissed one another, easily, gracefully, with no stretching or straining, Sakerson distinctly heard a soft smug sung sound.

"What's the matter?" Chiquita asked, sensing his distraction.

"I could have sworn . . . No, it couldn't be . . ."

"We're not to have secrets from each other."

He could sense that he'd better think quickly or lose the best thing that had happened to him. Then it occurred to him that when it came time to tell her the truth, he'd have the logged-on holo program to prove it. Right now was not the appropriate moment for that. He answered the immediate question.

"Part of a slogan, I guess." But Chiquita tilted her head, prompting him. "Something like . . . 'the lessons are free.'"

Introduction

When Steve and I decided in April to be the first kids on our block to publish a cold fusion story, we figured that the introduction could go one of two ways: a wry admission of jumping the gun vs. a mild gloating over getting there fustest with the mostest. It never occurred to us that at press time (early June) that the scientific community would have come to a negative consensus, and that the consensus would be wrong.

Well, so it has come to pass. P&F are exactly right in virtually all particulars and the scientific community is too blind (hysterical blindness is still blindness) to see. You read it here first.

ROACHSTOMPERS

S.M. Stirling

ABILENE, TEXAS
October 1, 1998
POST #72, FEDERAL IMMIGRATION CONTROL

"Scramble! Scramble!"

"Oh, shit," the captain of the reaction company said with deep disgust. It was the first time Laura Hunter had gotten past level 17 on this game. "Save and logoff."

She snatched the helmet from the monitor and stamped to settle her boots, wheeled to her feet and walked out of the one-time Phys-Ed teacher's office. One hand adjusted the helmet, flipping up the nightsight visor and plugging the comlink into the jack on her back-and-breast; the other snatched the H&K assault rifle from the improvised rack beside the door. Words murmured into her ears, telling the usual tale of disaster.

"All right," the senior sergeant bellowed into the echoing darkness of the disused auditorium they were using as a barracks. The amplified voice seemed to strike her like a club of air as she crossed the threshold. "Drop your cocks 'n grab your socks!"

It was traditional, but she still winced; inappropriate too, this was officially a police unit and thoroughly coed. "As you were, Kowalski," she said. The Rangers

Copyright © 1989 by S.M. Stirling

were tumbling out of their cots, scrambling cursing into uniforms and body-armor, checking their personal weapons. None of that Regular Army empty-rifle crap here. *Her* troopies were rolling out of their blankets ready to rock and roll, and *fuck* safety; the occasional accident was cheap compared to getting caught half-hard when the cucuroaches came over the wire.

Fleetingly, she was aware of how the boards creaked beneath their feet, still taped with the outlines of vanished basketball games. The room smelled of ancient adolescent sweat overlaid with the heavier gun-oil and body odors of soldiers in the field. *No more dances and proms here*, she thought with a brief sadness. Then data-central began coming through her earphones. She cleared her throat:

"Listen up, people. A and B companies scramble for major illegal intro in the Valley; Heavy Support to follow and interdict. Officers to me. The rest of you on your birds; briefing in flight. Move it!"

The six lieutenants and the senior NCO's gathered round the display table under the basketball hoop. They were short two, B company was missing its CO . . . no time for that.

"Jennings," she said. A slim good-looking black from Detroit, field-promoted, looked at her coolly; her cop's instinct said *danger*. "You're top hat for B while Sinclair's down. Here's the gridref and the grief from Intelligence; total illigs in the 20,000 range, seventy klicks from Presidio."

The schematic blinked with symbols, broad arrows thrusting across the sensor-fences and minefields along the Rio Grande. Light sparkled around strongpoints, energy-release monitored by the surveillance platforms circling at 200,000 feet. Not serious, just enough to keep the weekend-warrior Guard garrisons pinned down. The illigs were trying to make it through the cordon into the wild Big Bend country. The fighters to join the guerillo bands, the others to scatter and find enough to feed their children, even if it meant selling themselves as indentured quasi-slaves to the plains 'nesters.

"Shitfire," Jennings murmured. "Ma'am. Who is it this time?"

"Santierist Sonoran Liberation Army," she said. "The combatants, at least. We'll do a standard stomp-and-envelopment. Here's the landing-zone distribution. Fire-prep from the platforms, and this time be *careful*, McMurty. There are two thousand with small arms, mortars, automatic weapons, light AA, possible wire-guided antitank and ground-to-air heat-seekers."

"And their little dogs too," McMurty muttered, pushing limp blond hair back from her sleep-crusted eyes. "Presidio's in Post 72's territory, what're they—" She looked over the captain's shoulder "—sorry, sir."

Laura Hunter saluted smartly along with the rest; Major Forrest was ex-Marine and Annapolis. Not too happy about mandatory transfer to the paramilitary branch, still less happy about the mixed bag of National Guard and retread police officers that made up his subordinates.

"At ease, Captain, gentlemen. Ladies." Square pug face, traces of the Kentucky hills under the Academy diction, pale blue eyes. "And Post 72 is containing a major outbreak in El Paso. For which C and D companies are to stand by as reserve reinforcement."

"What about the RAC's? Sir." Jennings added. Forrest nodded, letting the 'Regular Army Clowns' pass: the black was more his type of soldier, and the corps had always shared that opinion anyway.

"This is classified," he said. "The 82nd is being pulled out of Dallas-Fort Worth."

"Where?" Hunter asked. Her hand stroked the long scar that put a kink in her nose and continued across one cheek. *That* was a souvenir of the days when she had been driving a patrol car in DC.

No more 82nd . . . It was not that the twin cities were that bad; their own Guard units could probably keep the lid on . . . but the airborne division was the ultimate reserve for the whole Border as far west as Nogales.

The Major made a considered pause. "They're staging through Sicily, for starters." Which could mean only one thing; the Rapid Deployment Force was heading for the Gulf. Hunter felt a sudden hot weakness down near the pit of her stomach, different and worse than the usual pre-combat tension.

Somebody whistled. "The Russian thing?" Even on the Border they had had time to watch the satellite pictures of the Caliphist uprisings in Soviet Asia; they had been as bloody as anything in the Valley, and the retaliatory invasion worse.

"COMSOUTH has authorized . . . President Barusci has issued an ultimatum demanding withdrawal of the Soviet forces from northern Iran and a UN investigation into charges of genocide."

"Sweet Jesus," Jennings said. Hunter glanced over at him sharply; it sounded more like a prayer than profanity.

"Wait a minute, sir," Hunter said. "Look . . . that means the RDF divisions are moving out, right?" All three of them, and that was most of the strategic reserve in the continental US. "Mobilization?" He nodded. "But the army reserve and the first-line Guard units are going straight to Europe? With respect, sir, the cucuroache—the people to the south aren't fools and they have satellite links too. Who the *hell* is supposed to hold the Border?"

The commander's grin showed the skull beneath his face. "We are, Captain Hunter. We are."

The noise in the courtyard was already enough to make the audio pickups cut in, shouts and pounding feet and scores of PFH airjets powering up. Pole-mounted glarelights banished the early-morning stars, cast black shadows around the bulky figures of the troopers in their olive-and-sand camouflage. The air smelt of scorched metal and dust. Hunter paused in the side-door of the Kestrel assault-transport, looking back over the other vehicles. All the latest, nothing too good for the Rangers—and they were small enough to re-equip totally on the first PFH-powered models out of the factories. Mostly Kestrels, flattened ovals of Kelvar-composite and reactive-armor panel, with stub wings for the rocket pods and chin-turrets mounting chain guns. Bigger boxy transports for the follow-on squads; little one-trooper eggs for the Shrike airscouts; the bristling saucer-shapes of the heavy weapons platforms.

She swung up into the troop compartment of her Kestrel, giving a glance of automatic hatred to the black rectangles of the PFH units on either side of the ceiling. "Pons, Fleischmann and Hagelstein," she muttered. "Our modern trinity." The bulkhead was a familiar pressure through the thick flexibility of her armor. "Status, transport."

"All green and go," the voice in her earphones said. "Units up, all within tolerances, cores fully saturated."

The headquarters squad were all in place. "Let's do it, then," she said. "Kestrel 1, lift."

The side ramps slid up with hydraulic smoothness, and the noise vanished with a soughing ching-*chunk*. Those were *thick* doors; aircraft did not need to be lightly built, not with fusion-powered boost. Light vanished as well, leaving only the dim glow of the riding lamps. There was a muted rising wail as air was drawn in through the intakes, rammed through the heaters and down through the swiveljets beneath the Rangers' feet. There were fifteen troopers back-to-back on the padded crashbench in the Kestrel's troop-compartment. One of them reached up wonderingly to touch a power unit. It was a newbie, Finali, the company comlink hacker. Clerk on the TOE, but carrying a rifle like the rest of them; the data-crunching was handled by the armored box on his back.

Hunter leaned forward, her thin olive-brown face framed by the helmet and the bill brow of the flipped-up visor. "*Don't—touch—that*," she said coldly as his fingers brushed the housing of the fusion unit.

"Yes ma'am." Finali was nearly as naive as his freckle-faced teenage looks, but he had been with A Company long enough to listen to a few stories about the Captain. "Ahh, ma'am, is it safe?"

"Well, son, they *say* it's safe." The boy was obviously sweating the trip to his first hot LZ, and needed distraction.

The transport sprang skyward on six columns of superheated air, and the soldiers within braced themselves against the thrust, then shifted as the big vents at the rear opened. The Kestrel accelerated smoothly toward its Mach 1.5 cruising speed, no need for high-stress maneuvers. Hunter lit a cigarette, safe enough on aircraft with no volatiles aboard.

"And it probably is safe. Of course, it's one of the doped-titanium anode models, you know? Saves on palladium. They kick out more neutrons than I'm comfortable with, though. Hell, we're probably not going to live long enough to breed mutants, anyway."

She blew smoke at the PFH units, and a few of the troopers laughed sourly.

"Captain?" It was Finali again. "Ah, can I ask a question?"

"Ask away," she said. *I need distraction too*. The tac-update was not enough, no unexpected developments . . . and fiddling with deployments on the way in was a good way to screw it up.

"I know . . . well, the depression and Mexico and everything is because of the PFH, but . . . I mean, I didn't even *see* one of them until I enlisted. It's going to be *years* before people have them for cars and home heating. How can it . . . how can it mess things up so bad *now*?"

Kowalski laughed contemptuously, the Texas twang strong in his voice. "Peckerwood, how much yew goin' to pay for a horse ever'one knows is fixin' to die next month?"

Finali flushed, and Hunter gave him a wry smile and a slap on the shoulder. "Don't feel too bad, trooper; there were economists with twenty degrees who didn't do much better." She took another drag on the cigarette, and reminded herself to go in for another cancer antiviral. *If we make it. Shut up about that*.

"Sure, there aren't many PFH's around, but we know they're going to be common as dirt; the Taiwanese are starting to ship out 10-Megawatt units like they did VCR's, in the old days. Shit, even the Mindanao pirates've managed to get hold of some. See, they're so simple . . . not much more difficult to make than a diesel engine, once Hagelstein figured out the theory. And you can do anything with them; heavy water in, heat or electricity or laser beams out. Build them any scale, right down to camp-stove size.

"Too fucking good, my lad. So all those people who'd been sitting on pools of oil knew they'd be worthless in ten, fifteen years. So they pumped every barrel they could, to sell while it was still worth something. Which made it practically worthless right away, and they went bust. Likewise all the people with tankers, refineries, coal mines . . . all the people who *made* things for anybody in those businesses, or who sold things to the people, or who lent them money, or . . ."

She shrugged. The Texan with the improbable name laughed again. "Me'n my pappy were roustabouts from way back. But who needs a driller now?"

"Could be worse," the gunner in the forward compartment cut in. "You could be a cucuroach."

That was for certain-sure. Hunter flipped her visor down, and the compartment brightened to green-tinted clarity. Mexico had been desperate *before* the discoveries, when petroleum was still worth something; when oil dropped to fifty cents a barrel, two hundred billion dollars in debts had become wastepaper. And depression north of the Border meant collapse for the export industries that depended on those markets, no more tourists . . . breadlines in the US, raw starvation to the south. Anarchy, warlords, eighty million pairs of eyes turned north at the Colossus whose scientists had shattered their country like a man kicking in an egg carton.

Fuck it, she thought. *Uncle Sugar lets the chips fall where they lie and gives us a munificent 20% bonus on the minimum wage for sweeping the consequences back into the slaughterhouse.*

The northern cities were recovering, all but the lumpenproletariat of the cores; controlled fusion had leapfrogged the technoaristocracy two generations in half a decade. Damn few of the sleek middle classes *here*, down where the doody plopped into the pot. Blue-collar kids, farm boys, blacks; not many Chicanos either. DC had just enough sense not to send them to shoot their cousins and the ACLU could scream any way they wanted; the taxpayers had seen the Anglo bodies dangling from the lampposts of Brownsville, seen it in their very own living rooms . . .

Without us, the cucuroaches would be all over their shiny PFH-powered suburbs like a brown tide, she thought, not for the first time. Strange how she had come to identify so totally with her troops.

"But as long as these stay scarce, we've got an edge," she said, jerking the faceless curve of her helmet toward the PFH. "Chivalric"

"Chivalric?" Finali frowned.

"Sure, son. Like a knight's armor and his castle; with that, we protect the few against the many." She pressed a finger against her temple. "Pilot, we coming up on Austin?"

"Thirty seconds, Captain."

"Take her down to the dirt, cut speed to point five Mach and evasive. Everybody sync." The cucuroach illigs could probably patch into the commercial satellite network—might have hackers good enough to tap the PFH-powered robot platforms hovering in the stratosphere. Knowing the Rangers were coming and being able to do anything about it were two separate things, though. As long as they were careful to avoid giving the war-surplus Stingers and Blowpipes a handy target.

The transport swooped and fell, a sickening express-elevator feeling. Hunter brought her H&K up across her lap and checked it again, a nervous tick. It too was the very latest, Reunited German issue; the Regulars were still making do with M16's. Caseless ammunition and a 50-round cassette, the rifle just a featureless plastic box with a pistol-grip below and optical sight above. They were talking about PFH—powered personal weapons, lasers and slugthrowers. Not yet, thank God. . . .

"30 minutes ETA to the LZ," the pilot announced. Hunter keyed the command circuit.

"Rangers, listen up. Remember what we're here for; take out their command-and-control right at the beginning. That's why we're dropping on their HQ's. Without that and their heavy weapons they're just a mob; the support people can sweep them back. We're *not* here to fight them on even terms; this is a roach stomp, not a battle." A final, distasteful chore. Her voice went dry:

"And under the terms of the Emergency Regulations Act of 1995, I must remind you this is a police action. All hostiles are to be given warning and opportunity to surrender unless a clear and present danger exists."

"And I'm King Charles V of bloody England," someone muttered.

"Yeah, tell us another fairy story."

"*Silence on the air!*" Top sergeant's voice.

Her mind sketched in the cities below, ghostly and silent in the night, empty save for the National Guard patrols and the lurking predators and the ever-present rats. Paper rustling down deserted streets, past shattered Arby's and Chicken Delights . . . out past the fortress suburbs, out to the refugee camps where the guards kicked the rations through the wire for the illig detainees to scramble for.

There would be no prisoners.

Very softly, someone asked: "Tell us about the island, Cap?"

What am I, the CO or a den mother? she thought. Then, *What the hell, this isn't an Army unit.* Which was lucky for her, the American military still kept women out of front-line service, at least in theory. The Rangers were a police unit under the Department of the Interior—also in theory. *And not many of the troopies ever had a chance at a vacation in Bali.*

Hunter turned and looked over the low bulkhead into the control cabin of the transport. Her mouth had a dry feeling, as if it had been wallpapered with Kleenex; they were right down on the deck and going *fast*. Kestrels had phased-array radar and AI designed for nape-of-the-earth fighters. Supposed to be reliable as all hell, but the sagebrush and hills outside were going past in a streaking blur. She brought her knees up and braced them against the seat, looking down at the central display screen. It was slaved to the swarm of tiny remote-piloted reconnaissance drones circling the LZ, segmented like an insect's eye to show the multiple viewpoints, with pulsing light-dots to mark the Ranger aircraft.

The Santierist guerrillas were using an abandoned ranch house as their CP. She could see their heavy weapons dug in around it, covered in camouflage net-ting. Useless, just patterned cloth, open as daylight to modern sensors . . . on the other hand, there weren't many of those in Mexico these days. Then she looked more closely. There were *mules* down there, with am-munition boxes on their backs. It was enough to make you expect Pancho Villa. A Santierist altar in the court-yard, with a few hacked and discarded bodies already thrown carelessly aside . . . *Voodoo-Marxist,* she thought. *Communal ownership of the spirit world. Time to tickle them.*

"Code Able-Zulu four," she said. Something in her helmet clicked as the AI rerouted her commlink. "Position?"

"Comin', up on line-of-sight," McMurty said. Weap-ons Section counted as a platoon, four of the heavy lifters with six troopers each.

There were lights scattered across the overgrown scrub of the abandoned fields beyond the ranch house, the numberless campfires of the refugees who had fol-lowed through the gap the Santierists had punched in the Border deathzone. Some of them might make it back, if they ran as soon as the firefight began.

Hunter reached out to touch half a dozen spots on the screen before her; they glowed electric-blue against the silvery negative images. "Copy?"

"Copy, can-do."

"Execute."

Another voice cut in faintly, the battalion AI prompter. "ETA five minutes."

"Executing firemission," the platform said.

The gamma-ray lasers were invisible pathways of energy through the night, invisible except where a luck-less owl vanished into a puff of carbon-vapor. Where they struck the soil the earth exploded into plasma for a meter down. It wasn't an explosion, technically. Just a lot of vaporized matter trying to disperse really, really fast. Fire gouted into the night across the cucuroach encampment, expanding outward in pulse-waves of shock and blast. She could hear the thunder of it with the ears of mind; on the ground it would be loud enough to stun and kill. The surviving AA weapons were hammering into the night, futile stabbing flickers of light, and. . . .

"Hit, God, we're hit!" McMurtry's voice, tightly controlled panic. The weapons platform was three miles away and six thousand feet up. Nothing should be able to touch it even if the cucuroaches had sensors that good. "Evasive—*Christ, it hit us again, loss of system integrity I'm trying to*—"

The voice blurred into a static blast. "Comm override, all Ranger units, *down*, out of line-of-sight, that was a zapper!"

The transport lurched and dove; points of green light on the screen scattered out of their orderly formation into a bee-swarm of panic. Hunter gripped the crashbars and barked instructions at the machine until a fanpath of probable sites mapped out the possible locations of the zapper.

"Override, override," she said. "Jennings, drop the secondary targets and alternate with me on the main HQ. Weapons?"

"Yes ma'am." McMurty's second, voice firm.

"Keep it low, sergeant; follow us in. Support with indirect-fire systems only." The weapons platforms had magneto-powered automatic bomb-throwers as well as their energy weapons.

"Override," she continued. "General circuit. Listen up, everyone. The cucuroaches have a zapper, at least one. I want Santicrist prisoners; you can recognize them by the fingerbone necklaces. Jennings, detach your first platoon for a dustoff on McMurtry."

"Ma'am—"

"That's a direct order, Lieutenant."

A grunt of confirmation. Her lips tightened; nobody could say Jennings didn't have the will to combat, and he led from the front. Fine for a platoon leader, but a company commander had to realize there were other factors in maintaining morale, such as the knowledge you wouldn't be abandoned just because everyone was in a hurry. Furthermore, Jennings just did not like her much. The feeling was mutual; he reminded her too strongly of the perps she had spent most of the early 90's busting off the DC streets and sending up for hard time.

"Coming up on the arroyo, Captain," the pilot said.

"Ready!" she replied.

The piloting screens in the forward compartment were directly linked to the vision-blocks in the Kestrel's nose; she could see the mesquite and rock of the West Texas countryside rushing up to meet them, colorless against the blinking blue and green of the control-panel's heads-up displays. The pilot was good, and there was nothing but the huge soft hand of deceleration pressing them down on the benches as he swung the transport nearly perpendicular to the ground, killed forward velocity with a blast of the lift-off jets and then swung them back level for a soft landing. The sides of the Kestrel clanged open, turning to ramps. Outside the night was full of hulking dark shapes and the soughing of PFH drives.

"Go!" Hunter shouted, slapping their shoulders as the headquarters team raced past. Getting troops out of armored vehicles is always a problem, but designing them so the sides fell out simplified it drastically. Cold high-desert air rushed in, probing with fingers that turned patches of sweat to ice, laden with dry spicy scents and the sharp aromatics of dry-land plants crushed beneath tons of metal and synthetic.

She trotted down the ramp herself and felt the dry, gravelly soil crunch beneath her feet. The squad was deployed in a star around her, comlink and display screen positioned for her use. The transports were lifting off, backing and shifting into position for their secondary gunship role as A company fanned out into the bush to establish a temporary perimeter. Hunter knelt beside the screen, watching the pinpoints that represented her command fanning out along two sides of the low slope with the ranch house at its apex.

"Shit, Captain," Kowalski said, going down on one knee and leaning on his H&K. She could hear the low whisper, and there was no radio echo, he must have his comm off. "That zapper one bad mother to face."

She nodded. Landing right on top of an opponent gave you a powerful advantage, and having the weapons platforms cruising overhead was an even bigger one. The zapper changed the rules; it was one of the more difficult applications of PFH technology, but it made line-of-sight approach in even the most heavily armored aircraft suicidal. Heavy zappers were supposed to be a monopoly of the Sovs and the US; having one fall into the hands of any sort of cucuroach was bad news. The Voodoo-Marxists . . . She shuddered.

Particularly if they had good guidance systems. Finali was trying to attract her attention, but she waved him to silence. "Too right, Tops. We'll just have to rush their perimeter before they can gather on the mountain."

SSNLF guerrillas were good at dispersing, which was essential in the face of superior heavy weapons. On the other hand, this time it kept them scattered. . . .

"Command circuit," she said. There was a subaudible click as the unit AI put her on general push. "Up and at 'em, children. Watch it, they've had a few hours to lay surprises."

There was little noise as the Rangers spread out into the sparse chest-high scrub, an occasional slither of boot on rock, a click of equipment. That would be enough, once they covered the first half-kilometer. Shapes flitted through the darkness made daybright by her visor, advancing by leapfrogging squad rushes. Almost like a dance, five helmeted heads appearing among the bushes as if they were dolphins broaching, dodging forward until they were lost among the rocks and brush. Throwing themselves down and the next squad rising on their heels . . .

"Weapons," she whispered. "Goose it."

"Seekers away," the calm voice answered her.

A loud multiple *whupping* sound came from behind

them, the air-slap of the magnetic mortar launch. A long whistling arc above, and the sharp *crackcrackcrack* of explosions. Mostly out of sight over the lip of the ravine ahead of them, indirect flashes against the deep black of the western sky. Stars clustered thick above, strange and beautiful to eyes bred among the shielding city lights. Then a brief gout of flame rising over the near horizon, a secondary explosion. Teeth showed beneath her visor. The seeker-bombs were homing on infrared sources: moving humans, or machinery; too much to hope they'd take out the zapper.

Time to move. She rose and crouch-scrambled up the low slope ahead of her. The open rise beyond was brighter, and she felt suddenly exposed amid the huge rolling distances. It took an effort of the will to remember that this was night, and the cucuroaches were seeing nothing but moonless black. *Unless they got nightsight equipment from the same sources as the laser*— She pushed the thought away.

"Mines." The voice was hoarse with strain and pitched low, but she recognized 2nd platoon's leader, Vigerson.

"Punch it," she replied, pausing in her cautious skitter.

A picture appeared in the center of the display screen, the silvery glint of a wire stretched across the clear space between a boulder and a mesquite bush. Jiggling as the hand-held wire-eye followed the metal thread to the V-shaped Claymore concealed behind a screen of grass, waiting to spew its load of jagged steel pellets into the first trooper whose boot touched it. Wire and mine both glowed with a faint nimbus, the machine-vision's indication of excess heat. Very recently planted, then, after being kept close to a heat-source for hours.

"Flag and bypass." *Shit, I hate mines*, she thought. No escaping them. The gangers had started using them in DC before she transferred. Bad enough worrying about a decapitating piano-wire at neck height when you chased a perp into an alley—but toward the end you couldn't go on a bust without wondering whether the door had a grenade cinched to the latch. That was how her husband had—another flight of magmortar shells

went by overhead; the weapons platform was timing it
nicely.

Think about the mines, not why she had transferred.
Not about the chewed stump of—think about mines.
Half a klick with forty pounds on her back, not counting
the armor. No matter how she tried to keep the individual loads down, more essentials crept in. Fusion-
powered transports, and they *still* ended up humping
the stuff up to the sharp end the way Caesar's knifemen
had. A motion in the corner of her eye, and the H&K
swept up; an act of will froze her finger as the cottontail
zigzagged out of sight. *Shit, this can't last much longer*,
she thought with tight control. They were close enough
to catch the fireglow and billowing heat-columns from
the refugee encampment beyond the guerilla HQ, close
enough to hear the huge murmur of their voices. Nobody was still asleep after what had already come down;
they must be hopping-tight in there.

Four hundred yards. The point-men must be on their
wire by now, if the Santierists had had time to dig in a
perimeter at all. For total wackos they usually had
pretty good sense about things like that and this time
there had been *plenty* of—

"Down!" somebody shouted. One of hers, the radio
caught it first. Fire stabbed out from the low rise ahead
of them, green tracer; she heard the thudding detonation of a chemical mortar, and the guerilla shell-burst
behind her sent shrapnel and stone-splinters flying with
a sound that had the malice of bees in it.

The Rangers hit the stony dirt with trained reflex,
reflex that betrayed them. Three separate explosions
fountained up as troopers landed on hidden detonators,
and there was an instant's tooth-grating scream before
the AI cut out a mutilated soldier's anguish.

"Medic, *medic*," someone called. Two troopers rushed
by with the casualty in a fireman's carry, back down to
where the medevac waited. Hunter bit down on a cold
anger as she toiled up the slope along the trail of
blood-drops, black against the white dust. The Santierists
were worse than enemies, they were . . . cop-killers.

"Calibrate," she rasped, "that mortar."

"On the way." A stick of seekers keened by over-head; proximity fused, they burst somewhere ahead with a simultaneous *whump*. Glass-fiber shrapnel, and anything underneath it would be dogmeat. Fire flicked by, Kalashnikovs from the sound of it, then the deeper ripping sound of heavy machine-guns. As always, she fought the impulse to bob and weave. Useless, and un-dignified to boot.

"Designators," she said over the unit push. "Get on to it."

This time all the magmortars cut loose at once, as selected troopers switched their sights to guidance. Nor-mally the little red dot showed where the bullets would go, but it could be adjusted to bathe any target a Ranger could see; the silicon kamikaze brains of the magmortar bombs sought, selected, dove.

"Come *on*!" she shouted, as the Santierist firing line hidden among the tumbled slabs of sandstone and thorn-bush ahead of them erupted into precisely grouped flashes and smoke. "*Now*, goddamit!" Fainter, she could hear the lieutenants and NCO's echoing her command.

The rock sloped down from here, down toward the ranch house and the overgrown, once-irrigated fields beyond, down toward the river and the Border. She leapt a slit-trench where a half-dozen cucuroaches sprawled sightless about the undamaged shape of an ancient M60 machine-gun; glass fragments glittered on the wet red of their faces and the cool metal of the gun. Then she was through into the open area beyond and the ruins of a barn, everything moving with glacial slowness. Running figures that seemed to lean into an invisible wind, placing each foot in dark honey. Shad-ows from the burning ruins of the farmhouse, crushed vehicles around it, her visor flaring a hotspot on the ground ahead of her and she turned her run into a dancing sideways skip to avoid it.

The spot erupted when she was almost past, and something struck her a stunning blow in the stomach. Air whoofed out of her nose and mouth with a sound halfway between a belch and a scream, and she fell to her knees as her diaphragm locked. Paralyzed, she could see the Claymore pellet falling away from her belly-armor, the front burnished by the impact that had flattened it. Then earth erupted before her as the mine's operator surged to his feet and levelled an AK-47, and that *would* penetrate her vest at pointblank range. He was less than a dozen yards away, a thin dark-brown young man with a bushy moustache and a headband, scrawny torso naked to the waist and covered in sweat-streaked dirt.

Two dots of red light blossomed on his chest. Fractions of a second later two H&K rifles fired from behind her, at a cyclic rate of 2,000 rounds a minute. Muzzle blast slapped the back of her helmet, and the cucuroach's torso vanished in a haze as the prefragmented rounds shattered into so many miniature buzzsaws.

"Thanks," she wheezed, as Finali and Kowalski lifted her by the elbows. "Lucky. Just winded." There would be a bruise covering everything between ribs and pelvis, but she would have felt it if there was internal hemorrhaging. A wet trickle down her leg, but bladder control was not something to worry about under the circumstances. She grabbed for the display screen, keyed to bring the drones down. The green dots of her command were swarming over the little plateau, and the vast bulk of the illigs further downslope showed no purposeful movement. Only to be expected, the Santeirists were using them as camouflage and cover. Which left only the problem of the—

Zap. Gamma ray lasers could not be seen in clear air, but you could hear them well enough; the atmosphere absorbed enough energy for that. The Rangers threw themselves flat in a single unconscious movement; Hunter cursed the savage wave of pain from bruised muscle and then ignored it.

"Get a fix, get a fix on it!" she called. Then she saw it herself, a matte-black pillar rising out of the ground like the periscope of a buried submarine, two hundred yards away amid artful piles of rock. *Shit, no way is a magmortar going to take that out,* she thought. It was too well buried, and the molecular-flux mirrors inside the armored and stealthed shaft could focus the beam anywhere within line of sight.

Zap. Half a mile away a boulder exploded into sand and gas, and the crashing sound of the detonation rolled back in slapping echoes. "Mark." Her finger hit the display screens. "Kestrel and Shrike units, thumper attack, repeat, thumper attack." The transports and airscouts would come in with bunkerbuster rockets. And a lot of them would die; as a ground weapon that zapper was clumsy, but it did *fine* against air targets . . .

"Damn, damn, *damn!*" she muttered, pounding a fist against the dirt. Another *zap* and the stink of ozone, and this time the gout of flame was closer, only a hundred yards behind them. Rocks pattered down, mixed with ash and clinker; back there someone was shouting for a medic, and there was a taste like vomit at the back of her throat. She groped for a thermite grenade—

"Captain."

It was Finali, prone beside her and punching frantically at the flexboard built into the fabric of his jacket sleeve. "Captain, I got it, I got it!"

"Got *what*, privat—"

There was no word for the sound that followed. At first she thought she was blind, then she realized the antiflare of her visor had kicked in with a vengeance. Even with the rubber edges snugged tight against her cheeks glare leaked through, making her eyes water with reaction. The ground dropped away beneath her, then rose up again and slapped her like a board swung by a giant; she flipped into the air and landed on her back with her body flexing like a whip. Hot needles pushed in both ears, and she could feel blood running from them, as well as from her nose and mouth. Above her something was showing through the blackness of the visor: a sword of light thrusting for the stars.

Pain returned, shrilling into her ears; then sound, slow and muffled despite the protection the earphones of her helmet had given. The jet of flame weakened, fading from silver-white to red and beginning to disperse. Stars faded in around it, blurred by the watering of her eyes; anybody who had been looking in this direction unprotected was going to be blind for a *long* time. It was not a nuclear explosion, she knew, not technically. There were an infinity of ways to tweak the anode of a PFH unit, and a laser-boost powerpack needed to be more energetic than most. Overload the charging current and the fusion rate increased exponentially, lattice energy building within the crystalline structure until it tripped over into instant release. There was a pit six yards deep and four across where the zapper had been, lined with glass that crackled and throbbed as it cooled. The rest of the matter had gone in the line of least resistance, straight up as a plasma cloud of atoms stripped of their electron shells.

"Finali?" Her voice sounded muffled and distant, and her tongue was thick. She hawked, spat blood mixed with saliva, spoke again. "Trooper, what the *hell* was that?"

"Deseret Electronuclear unit, Captain," he said, rising with a slight stagger. A cowlick of straw-colored hair tufted out from under one corner of his helmet; he pulled off the molded synthetic and ran his fingers through his curls, grinning shyly. "U of U design, access protocols just about like ours. I told it to voosh."

Kowalski fisted him on the shoulder. "Good work, trooper." There was a humming *shussh* of air as the first of the Kestrels slid over the edge of the plateau behind them. "You roasted their cucuroach *ass*, my boy!"

Hunter turned her eyes back to the display screen; motion was resuming. "There'll be survivors," she said crisply, looking up to the rest of the headquarters squad. "We'll—"

Crack. The flat snapping sound of the sniper's bullet brought heads up with a sharp feral motion. All except for Finali's; the teenager had rocked back on his heels, face liquid for a moment as hydrostatic shock rippled the soft tissues. His eyes bulged, and the black dot above the left turned slowly to glistening red. His body folded back bonelessly with a sodden sound, the backpack comlink holding his torso off the ground so that his head folded back to hide the slow drop of brain and blood from the huge exit wound on the back of his skull. There was a sudden hard stink as his sphincters relaxed.

Above them the Kestrel poised, turned. A flash winked from its rocket pods, and the sniper's blind turned to a gout of rock and fragments. Kowalski straightened from his instinctive half-crouch and stared down at the young man's body for an instant.

"Aw, shit, *no*," he said. "Not *now*."

"Come on, Tops," Hunter said, her voice soft and flat as the nonreflective surface of her visor. She spat again, to one side. "We've got a job of work to finish."

"In the name of the Mother of God, senora, have pity!" the man in the frayed white collar shouted thinly.

The cucuroach priest leading the illig delegation was scrawnier than his fellows, which meant starvation gaunt. They stood below the Ranger command, a hundred yards distant as the megaphone had commanded. Behind them the dark mass of the refugees waited, a thousand yards further south. That was easy to see, even with her visor up; the weapons platforms were floating overhead, with their belly-lights flooding the landscape, brighter than day. The Kestrels and Shrikes circled lower, unlit, sleek black outlines wheeling in a circuit a mile across, sough of lift-jets and the hot dry stink of PFH-air units.

Hunter stood with her hands on her hips, knowing they saw her only as a black outline against the klieg glare of the platforms. When she spoke, her voice boomed amplified from the sky, echoing back from hill and rock in ripples that harshened the accent of her Spanish.

"Pity on Santierists, old man?" she said, and jerked a thumb toward the ground. The priest and his party shielded their faces and followed her hand, those whose eyes were not still bandaged from the afterimages of the fusion flare. Ten prisoners lay on their stomachs before the Ranger captain, thumbs lashed to toes behind their backs with a loop around their necks. Naked save for their tattoos, and the necklaces of human fingerbone.

"Did they take pity on you, and share the meat of their sacrifices?"

The priest's face clenched: he could not be a humble man by nature, nor a weak one, to have survived in these years. When he spoke a desperate effort of will put gentleness into his voice; shouting across the distance doubled his task, as she had intended.

"These people, they are not Santierists, not diabolists, not soldiers or political people. They are starving, senora. Their children die; the warlords give them no peace. For your own mother's sake, let the mothers and little children through, at least. I will lead the others back to the border myself; or kill me, if you will, as punishment for the crossing of the border."

Hunter signaled for increased volume. When she spoke the words rolled louder than summer thunder.

"I GRANT YOU THE MERCY OF ONE HOUR TO BEGIN MOVING BACK TOWARD THE BORDER," the speakers roared. "THOSE WHO TURN SOUTH MAY LIVE. FOR THE OTHERS—"

She raised a hand. The lights above dimmed, fading like a theater as the curtains pulled back. *Appropriate,* she thought sourly. *If this isn't drama, what is?* A single spotlight remained, fixed on her.

"FOR THE OTHERS, *THIS.*" Her fist stabbed down. Fire gouted up as the lasers struck into the cleared zone before the mob, a multiple flash and crack that walked from horizon to horizon like the striding of a giant whose feet burned the earth.

The priest dropped his hand, and the wrinkles of his face seemed to deepen. Wordless, he turned and hobbled back across the space where a line of red-glowing pits stitched the earth, as neat as a sewing-machine's needle could have made. There was a vast shuffling sigh from the darkened mass of his followers, a sigh that went on and on, like the sorrow of the world. Then it dissolved into an endless ruffling as they bent to take up their bundles for the journey back into the wasteland.

Laura Hunter turned and pulled a cigarette from a pocket on the sleeve of her uniform. The others waited,

Jennings grinning like . . . what had been that comedian's name? MacDonald? Murphy? McMurty bandaged and splinted but on her feet, Kowalski still dead around the eyes and with red-brown droplets of Finali's blood across the front of his armor.

"You know," the Captain said meditatively, pulling on the cigarette and taking comfort from the harsh sting of the smoke, "sometimes this job sucks shit." She shook her head. "Right, let's—"

They all paused, with the slightly abstracted look that came from an override message on their helmet phones.

"Killed *Eisenhower*?" Jennings said. "You shittin' me, man? That dude been dead since before my pappy dipped his wick and ran."

Hunter coughed conclusively. "Not him, the *carrier*, you idiot, the ship." Her hand waved them all to silence.

". . . *off Bandar Abbas*," The voice in their ears continued. "*They*—" It vanished in a static squeal that made them all wince before the AI cut in. The Captain had been facing north, so that she alone saw the lights that flickered along the horizon. Like heat lightning, once, twice, then again.

"What *was* that, Cap?" Jennings asked. Even Kowalski looked to be shaken out of his introspection.

"That?" Hunter said very softly, throwing down her cigarette and grinding it out. "That was the end of the world, I think. Let's go."

"No. Absolutely not, and that is the end of the matter." Major Forrest was haggard; all of them were, after these last three days. But he showed not one glimpse of weakness; Hunter remembered suddenly that the commander of Post 73 had had family in Washington . . . a wife, his younger children.

She kept her own face impassive as she nodded and looked round the table, noting which of the other officers would meet her eyes. It was one thing to agree in private, another to face the Major down in the open.

The ex-classroom was quiet and dark. The windows had been hastily sealed shut with balks of cut styrofoam and duct tape. No more was needed, for now; four of the heavy transports were parked by the doors, with jury-rigged pipes keeping the building over pressure with filtered air that leached the chalk-sweat-urine aroma of school. Hunter could still feel the skin between her shoulder blades crawl as she remembered the readings from outside. The Dallas-Fort Worth fallout plume had come down squarely across Abilene, and she doubted there was anything living other than the rats within sixty miles.

She pulled on her cigarette, and it glowed like a tiny hearth in the dimness of the emergency lamp overhead. "With respect, sir, I think we should put it to a vote."

The blue eyes that fixed hers were bloodshot but calm; she remembered a certain grave of her own in DC whose bones would now be tumbled ash, and acknowledged Forrest's strength of will with a respect that conceded nothing.

"Captain," he said, "this is a council of war; accordingly, I'm allowing free speech. It is *not* a democracy, and I will not tolerate treason in my command. Is that clear?"

"Yes sir," she said firmly. "Without discipline, now, we're a mob, and shortly a dead one. Under protest, I agree, and will comply with any orders you give."

The ex-Marine turned his eyes on the others, collecting their nods like so many oaths of fealty. A few mumbled. Jennings grinned broadly, with a decisive nod.

"Dam' straight, sir."

"Well. Gentlemen, ladies, shall we inform the me—the troops?"

" 'tent-*hut!*"

The roar of voices died in the auditorium, and the packed ranks of the Rangers snapped to attention. A little raggedly, maybe, but promptly and silently. The officers filed in to take their places at the rear of the podium and Forrest strode briskly to the edge, paused to return the salute, clasped hands behind his back.

"Stand easy and down, Sergeant."

"Stand easy!" Kowalski barked. "Battalion will be seated for Major Forrest's address!"

The commander waited impassively through the shuffling of chairs, waiting for the silence to return. The great room was brightly lit and the more than four hundred troopers filled it to overflowing. But a cold tension hovered over them; they were huddled in a fortress in a land of death, and they knew it.

"Rangers," he began. "You know—"

Laura Hunter's head jerked up as she heard the scuffle from the front row of seats; one of the tech-sergeants was standing, rising despite the hissed warnings and grasping hands. She recognized him, from B Company. An ex-miner from East Tennessee, burly enough to shake off his neighbors. The heavy face was unshaven, and tears ran down through the stubble and the weathered grooves.

"You!" he shouted at the officer above him. "They're all dead, an' you did it! You generals, you big an' mighty ones. *You!*"

Hunter could feel Jennings tensing in the seat beside her, and her hand dropped to the sidearm at her belt. Then the hillbilly's hand dipped into the patch-pocket of his jacket, came out with something round. Shouts, screams, her fingers scrabbling at the smooth flap of the holster, the oval egg-shape floating through the air toward the dais where the commanders sat. Forrest turning and reaching for it as it passed, slow motion, she could see the striker fly off and pinwheel away and she was just reaching her feet. The Major's hand struck it, but it slipped from his fingers and hit the hardwood floor of the dais with a hard drum-sound. She could read the cryptic print on it, and recognized it for what it was.

Offensive grenade, with a coil of notched steel wire inside the casing. Less than three yards away. There was just enough time to wonder at her own lack of fear, *maybe the hormones don't have time to reach my brain*, and then Forrest's back blocked her view as he threw himself onto the thing. The *thump* that followed was hideously muffled, and the man flopped up in a salt spray that spattered across her as high as her lips. Something else struck her, leaving a trail of white fire along one thigh. She clapped a hand to it, felt the blood dribble rather than spout; it could wait.

In seconds the hall had dissolved into chaos. She saw

fights starting, the beginning of a surge toward the exits. It was cut-crystal clear; she could see the future fanning out ahead of her, paths like footprints carved in diamond for her to follow. She felt hard, like a thing of machined steel and bearings moving in oil, yet more alive than she could remember, more alive than she had since the day Eddie died. The salt taste of blood on her lips was a sacrament, the checked grip of the 9mm in her hand a caress. Hunter raised the pistol as she walked briskly to the edge of the podium and fired one round into the ceiling even as she keyed the microphone.

"*Silence.*" Not a shout; just loud, and flatly calm. Out of the corner of her eye she saw Jennings vault back onto the platform, leopard-graceful: later. "Sergeant, call to order."

Kowalski jerked, swallowed, looked at the man who had thrown the grenade as he hung immobile in the grip of a dozen troopers. " 'Tent—" his voice cracked. " 'Tent-*hut!*" he shouted.

The milling slowed, troopers looking at each other and remembering they were a unit. Shock aided the process, a groping for the familiar and the comforting. Hunter waited impassive until the last noise ceased.

"Major Forrest is dead. As senior officer, I am now in command in this unit. Any dispute?" She turned slightly; the officers behind her were sinking back into their chairs, hints of thought fighting up through the stunned bewilderment on their faces. All except Jennings. He gave her another of those cat-cool smiles, nodded.

"First order of business. You two; take that ground-sheet and wrap the Major's body, take it in back and lay it out on the table. Move." The two soldiers scrambled to obey. "Bring the prisoner forward."

Willing hands shoved the tech-sergeant into the strip of clear floor before the podium.

"Stand back, you others. Sergeant Willies, you stand accused of attempted murder, murder, and mutiny in time of war. How do you plead?"

The man stood, and a slow trickle of tears ran down his face. He shook his head unspeaking, raised a shaking hand to his face, lowered it. Hunter raised her eyes to the crowd; there was an extra note to their silence now. She could feel it, like a thrumming along her bones, a taste like iron and rust. *Be formal, just a little. Then hit them hard.*

"As commanding officer I hereby pronounce Sergeant Willies guilty of the charges laid. Does anyone speak in this man's defense?" Now even the sound of breathing died; the clatter of the two troopers returning from laying out the dead man's body seemed thunderloud. The spell of leadership was young, frail, a word now could break it. There would be no word; the certainty lifted her like a surfboard on the best wave of the season. She turned to the row behind her. "Show of hands for a guilty verdict, if you please?" They rose in ragged unison.

"Sergeant Willies, you are found guilty of mutiny and the murder of your commanding officer. The sentence is death. Do you have anything to say in your own defense?" The man stood without raising his face, the tears rolling slow and fast across his cheeks. Hunter raised the pistol and fired once; the big Tennessean pitched backward, rattled his heels on the floor and went limp. A trickle of blood soaked out from under his jacket and ran amid the legs of the folding chairs.

"Cover that," she said, pointing to the body. "We will now have a moment of silence in memory of Major Forrest, who gave his life for ours. Greater love has no man than this." Time to get them thinking, just a little. Time to make them feel their link to each other, part of something greater than their own fears. Give them something to lay the burden of the future on.

"Right." She holstered the pistol, rested her hands on her belt. "Major Forrest called you all together to give you the intelligence we've gathered and to outline our future course of action. There being no time to waste, we will now continue." Hunter kept her voice metronome-regular. "The United States has effectively ceased to exist."

A gasp; she moved on before the babble of questions could start. "The Soviets were on the verge of collapse a week ago, even before the Central Asian outbreak. They, or some of them, decided to take us with them. Their attack was launched for our cities and population centers, not military targets." *Which is probably why we're still here*. "The orbital zappers caught most of the ballistic missiles; they didn't get the hypersonic PFH-powered cruise missiles from the submarines just off-shore, or the suitcase bombs, and we think they've hit us with biological weapons as well. If there'd been a few more years . . ." She shrugged. "There wasn't."

"Here are the facts. We estimate half the population is dead. Another half will die before spring; it's going to be a long, hard winter. The temperature is dropping right now. Next year when the snow melts most of the active fallout will be gone, but there won't be any fuel, transport, whatever, left. You all know how close this country was to the breaking point before this happened, though we were on the way back up, maybe. Now it's going to be like Mexico, only a thousand times worse."

She pointed over one shoulder, southwards. "And incidentally, they weren't hit at all. We Border Rangers have held the line; try imagining what it's going to be like *now*."

Hunter paused to let that sink in, saw stark fear on many of the faces below. What had happened to the world was beyond imagining, but these men and women could imagine the Border down and no backup without much trouble. That was a horror that was fully real to them, their subconscious minds had had a chance to assimilate it.

"Some of the deeper shelters have held on, a few units here and there. Two of the orbital platforms made it through. I don't think they're going to find anything but famine and bandits and cucuroaches when they come back. Europe is hit even worse than we are, and so's Japan." She lit a cigarette. "If it's any consolation, the Soviets no longer exist."

"Major Forrest," she continued, "wanted us to make contact with such other units as survived, and aid in reestablishing order." Hunter glanced down at the top of her cigarette. "It is my considered opinion, and that of your officers as a whole, that such a course of action would lead to the destruction of this unit. Hands, if you please." This time she did not look behind her. "Nevertheless, we were prepared to follow Major Forrest's orders. The situation is now changed."

She leaned forward and let her voice drop. "We . . . we've been given a *damn* good lesson in what it's like trying to sweep back the ocean with a broom. Now we've got a tidal wave and a whisk."

A trooper came to her feet. "You're saying we're dead meat whatever we do!" Her voice was shrill; Hunter stared at her impassively, until she shuffled her feet, glanced to either side, added: "Ma'am," and sat.

"No. If we break up, yes, we're dead. Dead of radiation sickness, of cold, of plague, shot dead fighting over a can of dogfood."

Hunter raised a finger. "But if we maintain ourselves, as a fighting unit, the 72nd, we have a fighting chance, a *good* fighting chance. As a unit we have assets I doubt anyone on Earth can match. There are more than five hundred of us, with a broad range of skills. We have several dozen PFH-powered warcraft, fuel for decades, repair facilities, weapons that almost nobody outside the US and the Soviet can match, computers. *Most of all, we have organization.*"

She waited again, scanning them. *They're interested. Good.* "I just got through telling you we couldn't make a difference, though, didn't I?" Her hand speared out, the first orator's gesture she had made. "We can't make a difference *here*. Or even survive, unless you count huddling in a cabin in Wyoming and eating bears as survival. And I don't like to ski."

Feeble as it was, that surprised a chuckle out of them. "But we do have those assets I listed; what we need is a place where we can apply them. Where we won't be swamped by numbers and the scale of things. Where we can stand off all comers, try to make a life for ourselves. It won't be easy; we'll have to work and fight for it." The hand stabbed down. "*So what else is new?*"

A cheer, from the row where her old platoon sat. For a moment a warmth invaded the icy certainty beneath her heart, and then she pushed it aside. "A fight we can *win*, for a change. Better work than wasting illig kids and wacko cucuroach cannibals; and we'll be doing it for *ourselves*, not a bunch of fat-assed *citizens* who hide behind our guns and then treat us like hyenas escaped from the zoo!"

That brought them all to their feet, cheering and stamping their feet. The Border Rangers had never been popular with the press; few Rangers wore their uniforms when they went on furlough. Spit, and bags of excrement, sometimes outright murder not being what they had in mind. People with strong family ties avoided the service, or left quickly. She raised her hands for silence and smiled, a slow fierce grin.

"Right, listen up! This isn't going to be a democracy, or a union shop. A committee is the only known animal with more than four legs and no brain. You get just one choice; come along, subject to articles of war and discipline like nothing you've ever known, or get dropped off in a clear zone with a rifle and a week's rations. Which is it?"

Another wave of cheers, and this time there were hats thrown into the air, exultant clinches, a surf-roar of voices. *Hysteria,* she thought. *They'd been half-sure they were all going to die. Then they saw the murder. Now I've offered them a door—and they're charging for it like a herd of buffalo. But they'll remember.*

"I thought so," she said quietly, after the tumult. "We know each other, you and I." Nods and grins and clenched-fist salutes. "Here's what we're going to do, in brief. How many of you know about the Mindanao pirates?" Most of the hands went up. "For those who don't, they got PFH units, hooked them to some old subs and went a 'rovin'. After the Philippines and Indonesia collapsed in '93, they pretty well had their own way. A bunch of them took over a medium-sized island, name of Bali." Good-natured groans. "Yes, I know, some've you have heard a fair bit." She drew on the cigarette.

"But it's perfect for what we want. Big enough to be worthwhile, small enough to hold, with fertile land and a good climate. Isolated, hard to get to except by PFH-powered boost. The people're nice, good farmers and craftsmen, pretty cultured; and they're Hindu, while everyone else in the area's Muslim, like the corsairs who've taken over the place and killed off half the population. And I've seen the Naval intelligence reports; we can take those pirates. We'll be liberators, and afterward they'll still need us. No more than a reasonable amount of butt-kicking needed to keep things going our way." She threw the stub to the floor while the laugh died and straightened.

"Those of you who want to stay and take your chances with the cold, the dark and the looters report to First Sergeant Kowalski. For the rest, we've got work to do. First of all, getting out of here before we all start to glow in the dark. Next stop—a kingdom of our own! Platoon briefings at 1800. Dismiss."

" 'Tent-*hut*," Kowalski barked. Hunter returned their salute crisply, turned and strode off; it was important to make a good exit. Reaction threatened to take her in the corridor beyond, but she forced the ice mantle back. It was not over yet, and the officers were crowding around her.

"See to your people, settle them down, and if you can do it without obvious pressure, push the waverers over to our side. We need *volunteers*, but we need as many as we can get. Staff meeting in two hours; we're getting out tonight, probably stop over at a place I know in Baja for a month or so, pick up some more equipment and recruits. . . . Let's move it."

Then it was her and Jennings. He leaned against the stained cinderblock of the wall with lazy arrogance, stroked a finger across his mustache and smiled that brilliant empty grin.

"Objections, Lieutenant?" Hunter asked.

He mimed applause. "Excellent, Great White Raja-ess to be; your faithful Man Friday here just pantin' to get at those palaces an' mango trees and dancers with the batik sarongs."

Hunter looked him up and down. "You know, Jennings, you have your good points. You're tough, you've got smarts, you're not squeamish, and you can even get troops to follow you." A pause. "Good reflexes, too; you got off that dais as if you could see the grenade coming."

Jennings froze. "Say what?" he asked with soft emphasis. Hunter felt her neck prickle; under the shuck-and-jive act this was a very dangerous man. "You lookin' to have another court-martial?"

She shook her head. "Jennings, you like to play the game. You like to win. Great; I'm just betting that you've got brains as well as smarts, enough to realize that if we start fighting each other it all goes to shit and nobody wins." She stepped closer, enough to smell the clean musk of the younger soldier's presence, see the slight tensing of the small muscles around his lips. Her finger reached out to prod gently into his chest.

"Forrest was tough and smart too; but he had one fatal handicap. He was Old Corps all the way, a man of honor." There was enjoyment in her smile, but no humor. "Maybe I would have gone along with his Custer's Last Stand plan . . . maybe not. Just remember this; while he was living in the Big Green Machine, *I* was a street cop. I've been busting scumbags ten times badder than you since about the time you sold your first nickel bag. Clear, homes?"

He reached down with one finger and slowly pushed hers away. "So I be a good darky, or you whup my nigger ass?"

"Anytime, Jennings. Anytime. Because we've got a job to do, and we can't get it done if we're playing headgames. And I *intend* to get it done."

The silence went on a long moment until the Lieutenant fanned off a salute. "Like you say, Your Exaltedness. Better a piece of the pie than an empty plate. I'm yours."

She returned the salute. *For now*, went unspoken between them as the man turned away. Hunter watched him go, and for a moment the weight of the future crushed at her shoulders.

Then the Ranger laughed, remembering a beach, and the moon casting a silver road across the water. "You said I was fit to be a queen, Eddie," she whispered softly. "It's something to do, hey? And they say the first monarch was a lucky soldier. Why not me?"

The future started with tonight; a battalion lift was going to mean some careful juggling; there would be no indenting for stores at the other end. *But damned if I'll leave my Enya disks behind*, she thought, *or a signed first edition of* Prince of Sparta.

"Raja-ess," she murmured. "I'll have to work on that." She was humming as she strode toward her room. Sleet began to pound against the walls, like a roll of drums.

Introduction

For me, the test of a really first-rate story or article is whether it gives me a deeper insight into the world than I had before I read it. Even then, usually that insight is of a subtle sort, more often a reinforcement of current convictions that anything really new. While reviewing this article, however, I suddenly was gifted for the first time with a visceral understanding of how far it is to the nearest star. Thank you, Charles.*

*Since it isn't specifically mentioned in the article, let me share the insight: Take a meter stick. Take another. Place them side by side. Consider the first notch on the first stick: a millimeter. Contemplate it deeply. Got it? Good. Now step back and contemplate the two meters of the combined sticks. If the millimeter describes the limits of the Solar System, then the whole two meters will take you to Alpha Centauri. (If you want a visceral handle on how big the Solar System is, well, I'm still working on that.)

FLY ME TO THE STARS:
The Facts and Fictions of Interstellar Travel

Charles Sheffield

SIZING THE PROBLEM

To many people, travel to the stars may seem to be not much of a problem. After all (their logic goes) a dozen humans have already been to the Moon and back, the Soviet Union has serious plans for a crewed mission to Mars, probably soon after the turn of the century, and our unmanned probes have already allowed us to take a close look at every planet of the Solar System except Neptune and Pluto, with a Neptune flyby of the Voyager-2 spacecraft scheduled for August, 1989.

After interplanetary travel surely comes interstellar travel. The logical next step seems to be a manned or unmanned mission to one of the nearer stars. If we have been able to do so much in the thirty years since the world's space programs began, shouldn't such a stellar mission be possible in a reasonable time, say twenty or thirty years from now?

To answer that question, we must begin by sizing the problem. Then we can examine available technology, to see if and when we can hope for travel to one of the nearer stars.

Let us first examine distance scales. For travel here on Earth, different transportation systems are conveniently marked by factors of ten. Thus, for a distance up to two or three miles, most of us are willing to walk. For two to twenty miles, a bicycle is convenient and reasonable. A car or train is fine from twenty to two hundred, and above about three hundred miles most of us would rather fly than drive.

Once we move away from Earth, however, that convenient factor of ten is no longer useful. For example, the Moon is about 240,000 miles away, or 400,000 kilometers.* A factor of ten more than this does not take us anywhere interesting. Nor does a factor of a hundred. We have to use a factor of 1,000 to take us as far as the Asteroid Belt, and a factor of 10,000 to take us out to Voyager-2's location, between the orbits of Uranus and Neptune.

It is interesting to note that a factor of 10,000 *less* than the lunar distance, namely, 40 kilometers or 24 miles, is the sort of travel range that the average person had in his or her whole life, just a couple of centuries ago. We tend to think of the past in terms of Magellan and Columbus and Marco Polo, but most people lived and died close to their home town or village. And for much of the world this is still true today.

Ten thousand times the distance to the Moon takes

* In most of the discussion from this point on I will use metric units. Did you know that since the Metrication Act of 1974, the United States has in principle gone all-metric? In principle. Do you know your height in meters, or your weight in kilograms?

us 4 billion kilometers from Earth, to the outer planets of the Solar System, but it is a long way from taking us to the stars. For that we need *another* factor of 10,000. Forty trillion kilometers is about 4.2 lightyears, and that is very close to the distance of Alpha Centauri, the nearest star system to the Sun. (Alpha Centauri is actually a system of three stars orbiting about their common center of mass. Proxima Centauri, much the faintest of the three and the closest star to the Sun, is about 4.1 lightyears away, and the doublet pair of Alpha Centauri A and B is 4.3 lightyears away.) Thus the nearest star is about 100,000,000 times as far away as the Moon. The center of our galaxy, often visited in science fiction, is almost 10,000 times as far away again.

The numbers have little direct meaning to us. Perhaps a more significant way of thinking of the distance to the stars is to imagine that some genius were to develop a super-transportation system, one that could carry a spacecraft and its crew to the Moon in one minute. Anyone interested in solar system development will drool at the very thought of such a device. Yet that super-transportation system would take 190 years to carry its crew to Alpha Centauri—and this is our *nearest* stellar neighbor. Most of the stars that we think of as "famous" are much farther away: Sirius, the brightest star in the sky, is 8.7 lightyears distant, Vega 27 lightyears, Canopus (second brightest star in the sky) 98 lightyears, Betelgeuse about 520 lightyears, and the North Star, Polaris, over 600 lightyears. The system that takes us to the Moon in one minute needs 1,300 years to carry us to Vega, and over 20,000 years to reach Betelgeuse.

It will pay us to set our sights modestly. Let us ask for a system that takes us only as far as Alpha Centauri. We will leave the problem of reaching Canopus or Polaris for our descendants.

THE RULES OF THE GAME
We need to define terms a little more closely before we can fairly ask if Alpha Centauri is "within reach" of available technology. After all, the Pioneer-10 and 11

and the Voyager-1 and 2 spacecraft are already on trajectories that will take them clear out of the Solar System and eventually to the stars. They are already, in some sense of the word, interstellar missions. However, it will take them a long time to get there. Voyager-2, launched in 1977, will pass Neptune in 1989, and then fly free for hundreds of thousands of years before it reaches the distance of the nearest stars. Voyager-1 and the Pioneer spacecraft are embarked on equally long journeys.

This is not good enough. Let us require that a satisfactory system for interstellar travel must make the journey with its payload (not necessarily a human being) in one lifetime. We will assume a lifetime, somewhat arbitrarily and optimistically, to be one century.

Further, let us insist that any candidate spacecraft systems must be consistent with today's theories of physics. We will permit no "warp drives" or "hyperspace engines" or "space wormholes." More than that, we will not permit the use of entities, such as small rotating black holes, that are elements of today's physics, unless we can specify how to find or how to construct them.

These rules may be judged unduly restrictive. Technology will surely advance. The whole underpinnings of physical science may undergo radical revision, as they did at the beginning of this century with the coming of relativity and quantum theory. However, no one can predict the direction of those changes. And I would argue that if we cannot see how to do it *today*, with today's physics and technology, we should not try. We should wait for better techniques to come along.

TYPES OF SPACESHIP

Although there are dozens of different types of propulsion systems, they can be divided into two main types:

A) *Rocket Spaceships*, which achieve their motion via the expulsion of material (termed *reaction mass*) that they carry along with them or pick up as they travel. Usually, but not always, the energy to expel the reac-

tion mass comes from that reaction mass itself, by burning or through nuclear reactions.

B) *Rocketless Spaceships*, which neither carry nor
expel reaction mass.

The basic types that we will consider and evaluate
are as follows:

Rocket Spaceships	*Rocketless Spaceships*
1) Chemical rockets	10) Gravity swingby (not strictly a propulsion system, but highly valuable as we will see later)
2) Mass drivers	
3) Ion rockets	
4) Nuclear reactor rockets	
5) Pulsed fission rockets	
6) Pulsed fusion rockets	11) Solar sails
7) Matter/antimatter rockets	12) Laser beams
8) Photon rockets	There are also numerous permutations and combinations possible of these basic types, such as:
9) Bussard ramjet	
	13) Laser-heated reaction mass
	14) RAIR (Ram Augmented Interstellar Rocket)

PERFORMANCE MEASURES

We need one more thing before we can compare the
different systems available, and that is some method of
evaluating their performance. Rocket engineers have
such a widely-used measure, termed the *specific impulse*
(SI) of a rocket engine. It defines the performance of
the engine, as the length of time that one pound of
rocket fuel in that engine will produce a thrust of one
pound *weight*. Thus SI is a time, normally measured in
seconds.

For our purposes there are two things wrong with
using SI as a measure of system performance. First, in
addition to rockets we will be considering systems that
do not use reaction mass at all. Thus specific impulse
has no meaning in such cases. Second, it is hard to see
on theoretical grounds how big a value of SI might ever

be achieved. How can we determine the maximum specific impulse, possible with an ideal propulsion system, so as to produce relative performance figures for actual systems?

Instead of SI, we will therefore use a different performance measure, *effective jet velocity* (EJV). This is the effective velocity of the reaction mass as it is expelled. And we say effective velocity rather than actual velocity, because if the reaction mass is not expelled in the desired direction (opposite to the spacecraft's motion) the EJV will be reduced. Thus EJV measures both the potential thrust of a fuel, and also the efficiency of engine design.

The maximum possible value of EJV is easy to define. No velocity can ever exceed the speed of light, which is about 300,000 kilometers a second (actually, 299,792 kms/sec), and this is therefore the highest possible value of a system's EJV.

Conversion of EJV to SI is simple. In one second, a system with an EJV of V will need to expel g/V pounds of material to support a one-pound weight, where g is the gravitational acceleration at the surface of the Earth (0.00981 kms/second/second). One pound of fuel will thus be expelled in V/g seconds to support one pound of weight, and therefore the SI of a system is its EJV, divided by g. For example, an EJV of 10 corresponds to an SI of 1,019 seconds. We can now state the maximum possible value of SI. It is the speed of light divided by g, or 30,560,000 seconds.

EJV and SI are supremely important factors in spaceflight, because the ratio of final spacecraft mass (payload) to initial mass (payload plus fuel) depends *exponentially* on the EJV.

Explicitly, the relationship is $MI/MP = \exp(V/EJV)$, where MI = initial total mass of fuel plus payload,

MP = final payload mass, and

V = final spacecraft velocity.

(This is often termed the Fundamental Equation of Rocketry.)

In other terms, suppose that a mission has been designed in which the initial mass of payload plus fuel is

10,000 times the final payload. That is a prohibitively high value for most missions, and the design is useless. But if the EJV of the mission could somehow be doubled, the initial payload-plus-fuel mass would become only 100 (the square root of 10,000) times the final payload. And if it could somehow be doubled again, the payload would increase to one-tenth (the square root of 1/100) of the initial total mass. The secret to high-performance missions is high values of the EJV.

COMPARISON OF SYSTEMS

1) *Chemical rockets* using liquid hydrogen and liquid oxygen (LOX) as fuel can provide an EJV of maybe 4.3 kms/second. LOX plus kerosene gives an EJV of about 3, potassium perchlorate plus a petroleum product (solid fuel rocket) about 2. An EJV of 4.5 kms/second is probably the limit for chemical fuel rockets. To do any better than this, we would have to go to such exotic fuels as monomolecular hydrogen, which is highly unstable and dangerous.

The good news, of course, is that we know exactly how to build chemical rockets. Every launch that has ever been made was done with a chemical fuel rocket.

2) *Mass drivers* have usually been thought of as launch devices, throwing payloads to space using electromagnetic forces. They were originally proposed in 1950 by Arthur C. Clarke for launching payloads or construction materials from the surface of the Moon, and he called the device an electromagnetic sled launcher. The idea was worked out in more detail and actually built in prototype form on Earth by Gerard K. O'Neill and co-workers in the 1970s. They re-named it the mass driver.

A mass driver consists of a long solenoid with a hollow center. Pulsed magnetic fields are used to propel each payload along the solenoid, accelerating it until it reaches the end of the solenoid and flies off at high speed. As described here, the payload is the object that the mass driver is accelerating. However, if we invert our thinking, a mass driver in free space will itself be given an equal push by the material that is expelled (Newton's Third Law: Action and reaction are equal and opposite). If we think of the expelled material as reaction mass, then the long solenoid itself is part of the spacecraft, and will be driven along in space with the rest of the payload.

Ejecting a series of small objects using the mass driver can give an EJV to the mass driver itself of up to 8 kms/second. Such a device was proposed by O'Neill as an upper stage for the space shuttle, but never developed.

Note that 8 kms/second is almost double the EJV that can be achieved with chemical rockets, but note also that the energy to power the mass driver must be provided externally, as electricity generated from nuclear or solar power. The mass of such power-generation equipment will diminish the mass driver's performance as a propulsion system. In addition, the use of solar power works fine close to the Sun, but it would be a major problem in interstellar space. The available solar energy falls off as the inverse square of the distance from the Sun. We will encounter the same problem later, with other systems.

Again, the good news is that working mass drivers have been built. They are not just theoretical ideas.

3) *Ion rockets*. These are similar to mass drivers, in that the reaction mass is accelerated electromagnetically and then expelled. In this case the reaction mass consists of charged atoms or molecules, and the acceleration is provided by an electric field. The technique is the same as that used in the linear accelerators employed in particle physics work here on Earth. Very large linear accelerators have already been built; for example, the Stanford Linear Accelerator (SLAC) has an acceleration chamber two miles long.

SLAC is powered using conventional electric supplies. For use in space, the power supply for ion rockets can be solar or nuclear. As was the case with mass drivers, provision of that power supply will diminish system performance.

Prototype ion rockets have been flown in space. They offer a drive that can be operated for long periods of time, and thus they are attractive for long missions. They can produce an EJV of up to 70 kms/second, which is far higher than the EJV of either chemical rockets or mass drivers. Their biggest disadvantage is that they are low-thrust devices, providing just a few grams of thrust in their present forms. In order to achieve respectable final velocities of many kilometers per second, they must thus be operated for long periods of time, months or years, and they are certainly not useable to perform launches. They must rely on other types of propulsion to get them into space.

4) *Nuclear reactor rockets* use a nuclear reactor to heat the reaction mass, which is then expelled at high temperatures and at high velocities.

Systems with a solid core to the reactor achieve working temperatures up to about 2,500°C., and an EJV of up to 9.5 kms/second. Experimental versions were built in the early 1970s. Work on the most developed form, known as NERVA, was abandoned in 1973, mainly because of concern about spaceborne nuclear reactors. A solid core reactor rocket with hydrogen as reaction mass has an EJV more than double the best chemical fuel rocket, but the nuclear power plant itself has substantial mass. This reduces the acceleration to less than a tenth of what can be achieved with chemical fuels.

A liquid core reactor potentially offers higher performance, with a working temperature of up to 5,000°C. and an EJV of up to 25 kms/second. Gaseous core reactors can do even better, operating up to 20,000°C. and producing an EJV of 65 kms/second. However, such nuclear reactor rockets have never been produced, at least in the West, so any statements on capability are subject to question and practical proof.

5) *Pulsed fission rockets*. This is the first of the "advanced systems" that we will consider; advanced in the sense that we have never built one, and doing so might lead to all sorts of technological headaches; and also

advanced in the sense that such rockets, if built, could take us all over the solar system and out of it.

The idea for the pulsed fission rocket may sound both primitive and alarming. A series of atomic bombs (first design) or hydrogen bombs (later designs) are exploded behind the spacecraft, which is protected by a massive "pusher plate." This plate serves both to absorb the momentum provided by the explosions, and also to shield the payload from the radioactive blasts.

The pulsed fission rocket was proposed by Ulam and Everett in 1955. The idea, known as Project Orion, was investigated in detail between 1958 and 1965. It appeared practical, and it could have been built. However, the effort was abandoned in 1965, a casualty of the 1963 Nuclear Test Ban Treaty between the United States and the Soviet Union. Project Orion called for full-scale super-critical-mass atomic explosions, and the treaty made it difficult to test the proposed system. The EJV is excellent, up to 100 kms/second, but the mass of the pusher plate limited accelerations to a few centimeters/second/second (less than a hundredth of a gee). This is no good in a launch system, but it will achieve very respectable velocities over long periods. An acceleration of 1 cm/second/second (just over a thousandth of a gee) for one year produces an end speed of 310 kms/second. This, by the way, is far short of what we need for our interstellar mission. At 310 kms/second, a trip to Alpha Centauri takes 4,100 years.

6) *Pulsed fusion rockets*. The pulsed fission rocket of Project Orion has two big disadvantages. First, the nuclear explosions are full-scale nuclear blasts, each one equivalent in energy release to many thousands or even millions of tons of conventional explosives. Second, the massive "pusher plate" is useful as a protection against the blasts and as an absorber of momentum, but it greatly decreases the acceleration of the ship and the system efficiency.

The more recent designs of pulsed fusion rockets potentially overcome both these problems. Each fusion explosion can be a small one, involving only a gram or so of matter. The fusion process is initiated by a high-intensity laser or a relativistic electron beam focused on small spheres of the nuclear fuel. The resulting inward-traveling shock wave creates temperatures and pressures at which fusion can occur. Second, if the right nuclear fuels are used, all the fusion products can be charged particles. Their subsequent movement can therefore be controlled with electromagnetic fields, so that they do not impinge on the payload or on the walls of the drive chamber.

A very detailed analysis of a specific pulsed fusion rocket mission was performed by the British Interplanetary Society and published in 1978. Known as Project Daedalus, it was a mission design for a one-way trip to Barnard's Star, 5.9 lightyears from the Sun. This destination was preferred over the Alpha Centauri stellar system, because there seemed to be evidence of gravitational perturbations of Barnard's Star that suggested possible planets in orbit around it. The observational evidence that led to that conclusion has since been called into question, but the value of Project Daedalus is undiminished as a serious attempt to find a spacecraft design that permits an interstellar mission.

In Project Daedalus, small spheres of deuterium (D) and helium-3 (He3) were used as fusion fuels. (Deuterium is "heavy" hydrogen, with a neutron as well as a proton in the nucleus; helium-3 is "light" helium, which is missing a neutron in its nucleus.) The D-He3 reaction yields as fusion products a helium nucleus and a proton, both of which carry electric charges and can thus be manipulated by magnetic fields. The estimated EJV for Project Daedalus was 10,000 kms/second, leading to a fifty-year travel time for the 5.9 lightyear journey. The mass at launch from solar orbit was 50,000 tons, the final mass was 1,000 tons, and the terminal velocity for the spacecraft was one-eighth of the speed of light.

The design of this project was a technical *tour de force*, but the complications and caveats are significant. First, controlled pellet fusion of the type envisaged has not yet been demonstrated. The D-He3 fusion reaction in the fuel pellets proceeds rapidly only at extremely temperatures (700,000,000°C or higher), and achieving and containing such temperatures is a major problem. Other fusion reactions, such as deuterium-tritium, take place at a sixth of this temperature, but they produce uncharged neutrons as fusion products.

Third, and perhaps the biggest problem of all, the nuclear fuels needed are not available. Deuterium is plentiful enough, being present at one part in 6,000 in ordinary hydrogen. But He3 is very rare on Earth. The total U.S. supply is only a few thousand liters.

(I found this out the hard way. We wanted to buy some He3 for a scattering experiment at SLAC. The only commercial supplier was Monsanto, the price was prohibitively high, and the supply was limited. We worked out an odd solution. We *borrowed* the He3 that we needed from Monsanto, and returned it a year or so later as good as new—except that it had been bombarded with a highly relativistic electron beam.)

A few thousand liters is not enough for Project Daedalus. The design calls for 30,000 tons of the stuff, far more than could be found anywhere on Earth. The only place in the solar system where He3 exists in that sort of quantity is in the atmospheres of the gas-giant planets, Jupiter and Saturn and Uranus and Neptune. Project Daedalus proposed the use of a complicated twenty-year mining operation in the atmosphere of Jupiter, to be conducted by automated factories floating in the Jovian atmosphere. The construction of the spacecraft itself would be carried out near Jupiter.

The final report of Project Daedalus sets the time when a project like this might be carried out as roughly a century from now. If the design used for this project seems bizarrely complex and ambitious, remember that we are trying to travel 100,000,000 times as far as the Moon. Mind-boggling voyages are likely to need mind-boggling vehicles.

7) *Matter/antimatter rockets*. To every particle in nature there corresponds an anti-particle. Matter constructed from these anti-particles is termed antimatter or mirror-matter. For example, anti-hydrogen consists

of a positron moving about an anti-proton, whereas normal hydrogen is an electron moving about a proton.

When matter and antimatter meet, they annihilate each other. They therefore represent a vast source of potential energy.

If electrons and positrons meet, the result is high-energy gamma rays, and no particles. If protons and anti-protons meet, the result is between three and seven *pions*, elementary particles that come in two varieties, a charged form and an uncharged or neutral form. Neutral pions decay to form high-energy gamma rays in less than a thousand trillionth of a second. Charged pions last a lot longer, decaying to another elementary particle known as a *muon* in 25.5 nanoseconds. Muons decay in their turn to electrons and neutrinos, lasting on average 2.2 microseconds before they do so.

Neutrinos and gamma rays are difficult to convert to thrust, but charged particles are another matter. Proton-antiproton annihilation results in an average of three charged pions and two uncharged pions, with the charged pions carrying 60 percent of the total energy. The charged pions created in this process are traveling fast, at over ninety percent of the speed of light, and thus the effect of relativity is to increase their lifetime from 26 nanoseconds to 70 nanoseconds. This is more than long enough to control the movement of the charged pions with magnetic fields. Similarly, the rapidly-moving muons that appear as decay products last 6.2 microseconds before they in turn decay, and they too can be controlled through the use of magnetic fields.

Antimatter is a highly concentrated method of storing energy. The total energy produced by a milligram of antimatter when it meets and annihilates a milligram of ordinary matter is equal to that of twenty tons of liquid hydrogen/LOX fuel. It is therefore ideal for use on interstellar missions, where energy per unit weight is of paramount importance in fuels.

The most economical way of using such a potent fuel is not to take it "neat," but to dilute the antimatter with a large amount of ordinary matter. Matter/antimatter annihilation then serves to heat up the ordinary matter which is expelled as reaction mass. In this case, both the high-energy gamma rays and the pions serve to heat the reaction mass; and by choosing the antimatter/matter ratio, many different missions can be served with a single engine design. A highly dilute matter/antimatter engine has excellent potential for interplanetary missions.

Given all these useful properties of antimatter, one question remains: How do we get our hands on some of this good stuff?

That leads us to one of the major mysteries of physics and cosmology. There is as much reason for antimatter to exist as for ordinary matter to exist. Logically, the universe should contain equal amounts of each. In practice, however, antimatter is very rarely found in nature. Positrons and antiprotons occur occasionally in cosmic rays, but if we discount the highly unlikely possibility that some of the remote galaxies are all antimatter, then the universe is ordinary matter to an overwhelming extent.

One product of the recent inflationary models of the early universe is a possible explanation of the reason why there is so little antimatter. This, however, is of little use to us. We need antimatter now, and in substantial quantities, if we are to use matter-antimatter annihilation to take us to the stars.

Since antimatter is not available in nature, we will have to make our own. And this is possible. One byproduct of the big particle accelerators at Fermilab in Illinois, at IHEP in Novosibirsk in the Soviet Union, and at CERN in Switzerland, is a supply of antiprotons and positrons. The antiprotons can be captured, slowed down, and stored in magnetic storage rings. Antihydrogen can be produced, by allowing the antiprotons to capture positrons. Antimatter can be stored in electromagnetic ion traps, and safely transported in such containers.

We are not talking large quantities of antimatter with today's production methods. Storage rings have held up to a trillion antiprotons, but that is still a very small mass—about a trillionth of a gram. And antimatter needs a lot of energy to produce. The energy we will get from the antimatter will not be more than 1/10,000th of the energy that we put into making it. However, the concentrated energy of the end product makes this a unique fuel for propulsion.

The EJV of a matter/antimatter engine depends on the matter-to-antimatter ratio, and can be selected to match the needs of particular missions. However, for interstellar travel we can safely assume that we want the biggest value of the EJV that we can get. This will occur when we use a 1:1 ratio of matter to antimatter, and direct the charged pions (and their decay products, the muons) with magnetic control of their final emission direction. Since the charged pions contain 60% of the proton-antiproton annihilation energy, and since the uncharged pions and the gamma rays will be emitted in all directions equally, we find the maximum EJV to be 180,000 kms/second. With such an EJV, and a ratio of initial mass to final mass of 3:1, the terminal velocity of the mission will be almost two-thirds of the speed of light. We are in a realm of velocities where relativistic effects have a big effect on shipboard travel times.

8) *Photon rockets*. This takes the matter-antimatter rocket to its ultimate form, and also represents the ultimate in rocket spaceships that employ known physics.

A photon rocket assumes matter/antimatter annihilation, and further assumes that somehow *all* the resulting energy can be converted to thrust with 100 percent efficiency. This implies perfect magnetic control and re-direction of all charged pions, plus the control of all uncharged pions and gamma rays and of all decay products such as electrons and neutrinos. Every particle produced in matter-antimatter annihilation ultimately decays to radiation, or to electrons and positrons that can then annihilate each other to give pure radiation. If all this radiation can be emitted as a tightly collimated beam in a direction opposite to the spacecraft's motion, the resulting EJV will be the speed of light.

If a chemical rocket with a fuel-to-payload ratio of 10,000:1 could be replaced with a photon rocket, the mission would be 99.99 percent payload, and the fuel would be a negligible part of the total mass. Having said that, we must also say that we have no idea how to make a photon rocket. It could exist, according to today's physics, and it is quite impossible with today's technology.

9) *Bussard ramjet*. This is a concept introduced by Robert Bussard in 1960. A "scoop" in front of the spaceship funnels interstellar matter into a long hollow cylinder that comprises a fusion reactor. The material collected by the scoop undergoes nuclear fusion, and the reaction products are emitted at high temperature and velocity from the end of the cylinder opposite to the scoop, to propel the spacecraft. The higher the ship's speed, the greater the rate of supply of fuel, and thus the greater the ship's acceleration.

It is a wonderfully attractive idea, since it allows us to use reaction mass without ever worrying about carrying it along with us. There is interstellar matter everywhere, even in the "emptiest" reaches of open space.

Now let us look at the "engineering details."

First, it will be necessary to fuse the fuel on the fly, rather than forcing it to accelerate until its speed matches the speed of the ship. Otherwise, the drag of the collected fuel will slow the ship's progress. Such a continuous fusion process calls for a very unusual reactor, long enough and operating at pressures and temperatures high enough to permit fusion while the collected interstellar matter is streaming through the chamber.

Second, interstellar matter is about two-thirds hydrogen, one-third helium, and negligible proportions of other elements. Also, the fusion of helium is a complex process that calls for three helium nuclei to interact and form a carbon nucleus. Thus the principal fusion reaction of the Bussard ramjet will be proton-proton fusion (the nucleus of the hydrogen atom is a proton). Fusion of protons is hindered by the charge of each proton, which repels them away from each other. Thus pressures and temperatures in the fusion chamber must be high enough to overcome that mutual repulsion. Proton-proton fusion needs working temperatures of at least tens of millions of degrees, and there is a trade-off between the operating temperature of the fusion chamber, and its necessary length for protons to be within it long enough to fuse.

Third, there is roughly one atom of interstellar matter in every cubic centimeter. Thus, the matter scoop will have to be many thousands of kilometers across if the available hydrogen is to be supplied in enough quantity to keep a fusion reaction going. It is impractical to construct a material scoop of such a size, so we will be looking at some form of scoop that uses magnetic fields. Unfortunately, the hydrogen of interstellar space is mainly *neutral* hydrogen, i.e. a proton with an electron moving around it. Since we need a charged material in order to be able to collect it electromagnetically, some method must be found to ionize the hydrogen, i.e. to strip the electron away from the proton. This can be done using lasers that beam their radiation at a carefully selected wavelength out ahead of the Bussard ramjet. It is not clear that a laser can be built that requires less energy than is provided by the fusion process. It is also not clear that materials exist strong enough to permit construction of a magnetic scoop with the necessary field strengths.

As I said, the Bussard ramjet is a beautiful concept. However, for the reasons listed above I am sceptical that a working model can be built within the next couple of centuries.

SUMMARY OF ROCKET SPACESHIPS

We have examined systems with EJV's ranging from the 4.3 kms/second of chemical rockets to the 300,000 kms/second of photon rockets. They also range from the completely practical, in terms of today's manufacturing capability, to the totally impractical and maybe impossible.

If this country or the whole world were to embark on a crash effort to build a starship, similar to the World War Two "Manhattan Project" that led to the first atomic bomb, which of the rocket spacecraft that we have described could be produced? Let us give ourselves twenty years to make it, and assume that development of a space manufacturing and construction capability proceeds in parallel with design and construction of the interstellar spacecraft.

My conclusion is that we would be unlikely to do better than a pulsed fission rocket, or a pulsed fusion rocket powered by fission-triggered hydrogen bombs. Even if we mastered the micro-fusion technology needed to induce fusion with lasers or electron beams, a pulsed fusion rocket, Project Daedalus-style, would lack the necessary He3 fuel supply. We could not mine it from Jupiter in twenty years. Similarly, even if we knew how to handle matter-antimatter reaction products in a sophisticated manner, we would lack an adequate anti-matter supply. The Bussard ramjet also calls for engineering far beyond today's capabilities.

The EJV of our pulsed fission or pulsed macro-fusion rocket might be as much as 300 kms/second. Assuming a fuel-to-payload ratio of 10,000:1 (this is very large by today's mission planning standards; Project Daedalus had a 50:1 ratio), the final velocity of the ship would be 2,760 kms/second, which is a little less than one percent of the speed of light. Travel time to Alpha Centauri would be 470 years.

We have flunked, according to the rules that we set up earlier in the article. Now we must examine rocketless spacecraft, to see if they offer better prospects of success.

MORE COMPARISONS: ROCKETLESS SYSTEMS
The central problem for the rocket spacecraft that we can build today and in the near future is easy to identify. For small EJV's (which I will for our purposes define as less than 1,000 kms/second—a value which would make any of today's rocket engineers ecstatic) most of the reaction mass does not go to accelerate the payload. It goes to accelerate *the rest of the fuel*. This is particularly true in the early stages of the mission, when the rocket may be accelerating an initial thousand tons of fuel in order to provide a final acceleration to ten tons of payload. All systems which carry their reaction mass along with them suffer this enormous intrinsic disadvantage.

It seems plausible, then, that systems which do not employ reaction mass at all may be the key to successful interstellar travel. We will now examine such systems.

10) *Gravity swingby.* There is one form of velocity increase that needs neither onboard rockets nor an external propulsion source. In fact, it can hardly be called a propulsion system in the usual sense of the word. If a spacecraft flies close to a planet it can, under the right circumstances, obtain a velocity boost from the planet's gravitational field. This technique is used routinely now in interplanetary missions, and was employed in permitting Pioneer-10 and 11 and Voyager-1 and 2 to escape from the solar system completely. Jupiter, the biggest planet of the system with a mass 318 times that of Earth, can give a velocity kick of up to 30 kms/second to a passing spacecraft. So far as the spaceship is concerned, there will be no feeling of onboard acceleration as the speed increases. An observer on the ship would continue to feel as though in free-fall, even while accelerating relative to the Sun.

If onboard fuel is available to produce a velocity change, another type of swingby can do even better. This involves a close approach to the Sun, rather than to one of the planets, and the trick is to swoop in very near to the solar surface and then apply all the available thrust while at perihelion, the point of closest approach.

Suppose that your ship has a very small velocity far from the Sun. Allow it to drop towards the Sun, so that it comes close enough almost to graze the solar surface. When it is at its closest, suppose that there is enough onboard fuel to give you a 10 kms/second kick in speed; then your ship will move away and leave the solar system completely, with a terminal velocity far from the Sun of 110 kms/second.

The question that inevitably arises with such a boost at perihelion is, where did that "extra" energy come from? If the velocity boost had been given without swooping in close to the Sun, the ship would have left the solar system at 10 kms/second. Simply by arranging that the same boost be given very near to the Sun, the ship leaves at 110 kms/second. And yet the Sun has done no work. The solar energy has not decreased at all.

The answer to this puzzle is a simple one, but it leaves many people worried. It is based on the fact that kinetic energy changes as the square of velocity, and it runs as follows:

The Sun increases the speed of the spacecraft during its run towards the solar surface, so that our ship, at rest far from Sol, will be moving at 600 kms/second as it sweeps past the solar photosphere. Kinetic energy of a body with velocity V is $\frac{1}{2}V^2$ per unit mass, so for an object moving at 600 kms/second, a 10 kms/second velocity boost increases the kinetic energy per unit mass by $\frac{1}{2}(610^2-600^2) = 6,050$ units. If the same velocity boost had been used to change the speed from 0 to 10 kms/second, the change in kinetic energy per unit mass would have been only 50 units. Thus by applying our speed boost at the right moment, when the velocity is already high, we can increase the energy change by a factor of $6,050/50 = 121$, which is equivalent to a factor of 11 (square root of 121) in final speed. Our 10 kms/second boost has been transformed to a 110 kms/second boost.

All that the Sun has done to the spaceship is to change the speed *relative to the Sun* at which the velocity boost is applied. The fact that kinetic energy goes as the square of velocity does the rest.

This seems to be getting something for nothing, and in a way it is. Certainly, no penalty is paid for the increased velocity, except for the possible danger of sweeping in that close to the Sun's surface. And the closer that one can come to the center of gravitational attraction when applying the velocity boost, the more gratifying the result. One cannot go closer to the Sun's center without hitting the solar surface, but an approach to within 20 kilometers of the center of a neutron star of solar mass, for example, would convert a 10 kms/second velocity boost to a final departure speed from the neutron star of over 1,500 kms/second. (In such a case, though, tidal forces of over 10,000,000 gees might leave the passengers a little the worse for wear.)

Suppose one were to perform the swingby with a

speed much greater than that obtained by falling from rest towards the Sun. Would the gain in velocity be greater? Unfortunately, it works the other way round. The gain in speed is maximum if you fall in with zero velocity when a long way away. The biggest boost you can obtain from your 10 kms/second velocity kick is an extra 100 kms/second. That's not fast enough to take us to Alpha Centauri in a hurry. A speed of 110 kms/second implies a travel time of 11,800 years.

11) *Solar sails*. Gravity swingby of the Sun or Jupiter can't take us to the stars in a time that satisfies our own requirements. However, the Sun is also a continuous source of a possible propulsive force, namely, solar radiation pressure. Why not build a large sail to accelerate a spacecraft by simple photon pressure?*

We know from our own experience that sunlight pressure is a small force—we don't have to "lean into the sun" to stay upright. Thus a sail of large area will be needed, and since the pressure has to accelerate the sail as well as the payload, we must use a sail of very low mass per unit area.

The thinnest, lightest sail that we can probably make today is a hexagonal mesh with a mass of 0.11 grams/square meter. Assuming that the payload masses a lot less than the sail itself, a ship with such a solar sail would accelerate away from Earth orbit to interstellar regions at 0.01 gees.

This acceleration diminishes farther from the Sun, since the radiation pressure per unit area falls off as the inverse square of the distance. A solar sail starting at 0.01 gees at Earth orbit will be out past Neptune in one year, 5 billion kilometers from the Sun and traveling at 170 kms/second. Travel time to Alpha Centauri would be 7,500 years, and light pressure from the target star could be used to slow the sail in the second half of the flight.

12) *Laser beam propulsion*. If the acceleration of a solar sail did not decrease with distance from the Sun, the

* The "solar wind" pressure from particles emitted from the Sun is small compared with radiation pressure from photons.

same sail considered in the last section would have traveled ten times as far in one year, and would be moving at 3,100 kms/second. This prompts the question, can we provide a *constant* force on a sail, and hence a constant acceleration, by somehow creating a tightly focused beam of radiation that does not fall off with distance?

Such a focused beam is provided by a laser or a maser, and this idea has been explored extensively by Robert Forward. In his most ambitious design, a laser or maser beam is generated using the energy of a large solar power satellite near the orbit of Mercury. This is then sent to a transmitter lens, hanging stationary out between Saturn and Uranus. This lens is of Fresnel ring type, 1,000 kilometers across, with a mass of 560,000 tons. It can send a laser beam 44 lightyears without significant beam spreading, and in Forward's design a circular lightsail with a mass of 80,000 tons and a payload of 3,000 tons can be accelerated at that distance at 0.3 gees. That is enough to move the sail at half the speed of light in 1.6 years.

Forward also offers an ingenious way of stopping the sail at its destination, and then returning it to the vicinity of the Sun. The circular sail is constructed in discrete rings, like an archery target. As the whole sail approaches its destination, one inner circle, 320 kilometers across and equal in area to one-tenth of the original sail, is separated from the outer ring. Reflected laser light from the outer ring now serves to slow and halt the inner portion at the destination star, while the outer ring flies on past, still accelerating. When exploration of the target stellar system is complete, an inner part of the inner ring, 100 kilometers across and equal in area to one-tenth of the whole inner ring, is separated from the rest. This "bull's-eye" is now accelerated back towards the Sun, using reflected laser beam pressure from the outer part of the original inner ring. Finally, the direct laser beam will slow the bull's-eye when it returns to the Sun. The travel time to Alpha Centauri, including slowing-down and stopping when we arrive, is very acceptable, being 8.6 years (Earth time) and 7 years (shipboard time). Note that we have reached speeds where relativistic effects make a significant difference to perceived travel times. The ship's maximum speed before deceleration begins is four-fifths of the speed of light.

Now for the key question. Could we build such a ship, assuming an all-out worldwide effort and a timetable of, say thirty years?

Not yet. The physics is all fine, but the engineering would totally defeat us. The power requirement of the laser beam is many thousands of times greater than the total electrical production of all the nations on Earth. The implied space construction capability is also generations ahead of what can reasonably be projected for the next twenty or thirty years. We are not likely to go to the stars this way—something better will surely come along before we are ready to do it.

HYBRID SYSTEMS

Since neither rocket spacecraft nor rocketless spacecraft can take us to the nearest star as fast as we would like to go there, our only hope is with some kind of hybrid system. The two main candidates worth considering were already mentioned, namely, a laser-heated rocket, and a ram augmented interstellar rocket (RAIR).

13) The *laser-heated rocket* carries reaction mass, but that mass does not have to provide the energy for its own expansion. The energy is provided by a power laser, which can be a considerable distance from the target spaceship. This concept was proposed by Arthur Kantrowitz as a technique for spacecraft launch, and it is also being evaluated as a power source for aircraft. It is also attractive for interplanetary missions.

As an interstellar system, however, it suffers the defects of both the rocket and the rocketless spacecraft. Much of the reaction mass is wasted in accelerating the rest of the reaction mass; and for the laser power to be available at interstellar distances, it would be necessary to build a massive in-space power laser system. And even when all of this has been done, the EJV will not exceed maybe 200 kms/second. It is not a suitable tool for interstellar missions.

14) The *RAIR* employs a Bussard ramscoop, to collect interstellar matter. However, instead of fusing such matter as it flashes past the ship, in the RAIR an onboard fusion reactor with its own fusion materials is used to heat the collected hydrogen and helium, which then exits the RAIR cylinder at high speed.

Certainly, this eliminates one of the central problems of the Bussard ramjet, namely, that of fusing hydrogen quickly and efficiently, and it also allows us to make use of interstellar helium. However, the other problems of the Bussard ramjet still exist. It is necessary to ionize the interstellar medium, prior to collecting it in the magnetic scoop, and the design of the scoop itself presents lots of problems. It is highly unlikely that we could build a working RAIR in a generation, even with an all-out effort. One little-mentioned problem with both the RAIR and the original Bussard ramjet is the need to reach a certain speed before the fusion process can begin, since below that speed there will not be enough material delivered to the fusion system. The acceleration to reach that minimum velocity is itself beyond today's capabilities.

CONCLUSION

A friend of mine who works for the U.S. Commerce Department served recently on an evaluation team of grant applications. To be given serious consideration, an application must score eight or more out of a possible ten.

The evaluation team consists of fifteen people, and they take turns being the first one to comment. When Dutch (that's my friend) had his turn, he was asked what score he would give to a particular new grant application.

"I give it a two," he said.

At that point, a man at the other end of the table objected. He then took ten minutes of everyone's time, pointing out that there were virtues in the application that Dutch seemed to have overlooked completely, and that a score of only two was not fair. When he seemed ready to go on forever, Dutch felt that more than enough time had been taken by the one grant application.

"All right," he finally said. "You don't like my score. What score would *you* give it?"

The other man paused and thought. "I would give it a three," he said.

At the moment, I feel a bit like that man. Having set ground rules for interstellar flight, I have led you all this way and wasted all your time, only to tell you that no system available today or in the near future will permit interstellar travel according to my own self-imposed rules. Everything we have looked at either exceeds today's technological capacities, or it won't get us there in less than a thousand years.

And yet I do not feel apologetic. What we have found, for many different systems, is that we have the physical knowledge to permit interstellar travel with a trip time of a century; what we don't have, by a big margin, is the technological infrastructure to let us do what our science tells us is physically possible. In particular, we don't have enough energy available, and we don't have an established in-space presence and manufacturing capability.

This is not cause for great discouragement. If history is any guide, we will see available energy multiply by orders of magnitude in the next century or two, and space development will flourish over the same period. We tend to be impatient with the slow pace of the space program, but from a historical point of view humans are bursting off this planet and into space. The space-based projects that I have described, which today may seem so daunting and over-ambitious, won't make our descendants turn a hair. Think how Columbus would have reacted to a design for a Boeing 747, or worse yet, a space shuttle.

Interstellar travel is a real possibility for the future; but it will be the future of our great-grandchildren, not us or our children.

Introduction

In this latest installment from The Man-Kzin Wars, *the question of what constitutes ugly on an ape becomes crucial. And we are not talking about the pseudo-profundity that beauty is only skin deep; that, after all, depends on the beholder.*

BRIAR PATCH

Dean Ing

SYNOPSIS OF PART ONE

At the start of the Fourth Man–Kzin war, huge tigerish Kzin warriors capture a human ethologist, Locklear,
who is studying animal life near the rim of Known
Space. The Kzinti discover a brown dwarf with a single
synthetic planet that seems designed as an enormous
zoo, with habitat compounds separated by transparent
force cylinders. The ferocious but ethical commander,
"Scarface," leaves Locklear in a compound that copies
the Kzin homeworld. Locklear calls the planet "Zoo,"
and this compound "Kzersatz;" he can see an earthlike
compound tantalizingly near, through the force walls,
and calls it "Newduvai."

Locklear discovers ancient Kzinti and their animals in
a stasis crypt, and releases a few females including the
sleek, sexy Kit. Loyal to Locklear, they help fight the
returning team of warriors and only Scarface, bedazzled
by Kit, is taken alive.

Although the Man–Kzin war is in full swing elsewhere, Locklear ". . . ain't gonna study war no more,"
and negotiates a truce with Scarface, knowing that a
Kzin warrior is a cat of his word. The mating of Kit and

Scarface makes Locklear admit he itches for a loving woman. Leaving Scarface to decide whether to release the dozens of ancient Kzinti still in stasis, Locklear takes the Kzin lifeboat and makes the suborbital jump over the force walls to explore Newduvai.

Newduvai is a copy of an Eastern Mediterranean region and its stasis crypt contains Ice-Age animals—including mammoths, aurochs, and Neanderthals! Locklear releases them and dubs his favorite, a homely, gentle, buxom female, "Ruth." He soon learns why Neanderthals learn modern speech so quickly: they are mildly telepathic. They have no inhibitions about sex, but many about killing because the quarry's death is painful to telepaths.

He hides the Kzin lifeboat, fearing another visit by modern Kzinti, and by now he knows how to use the gravity-polarizer units from stasis cages to build a raft-like air scooter. Locklear's life in a hut with Ruth is made exasperating by a teen-aged girl, Loli, whose features are not Neanderthal but modern. The Neanderthals clearly understand that Loli and Locklear are not "gentles" like themselves, but "new" people. And like all new people, Loli is no telepath.

The other Neanderthals build a village and, furious at catching a young man and Ruth enjoying each other, Locklear sends Ruth to the village. He misses her but, to counter his memories of her, reminds himself that she was mud-ugly by modern standards. The villagers can forage nicely without meat if they choose and Locklear forbids them to kill game until it multiplies, knowing they could quickly kill off important species. The villagers can't understand this, and continue to hunt. Locklear returns in a rage, wanting to kill someone but with no intention of doing it. They sense his hostility and, sobbing, Ruth warns him to leave the village instantly. Gentles only kill when they must, but Locklear may qualify as a "must."

The girl, Loli, is too young for Locklear's taste and partly because of that, she prefers Locklear to the randy Neanderthal men. She warns him to be wary of pit traps and now Locklear realizes he would be almost as well-off on Kzersatz.

Then a cruiser thunders into Newduvai shooting, an Interworld Commission ship crewed by six men and a woman. Curt Stockton, Commander of the *Anthony Wayne*, apologizes to Locklear for firing on the Neanderthal village; he had mistaken them for Kzinti, and this is wartime. The *Wayne*, says Stockton, was detailed to these coordinates to recover some unspecified military secret found in Kzin records.

Locklear laughs: "Probably it was me," he admits. After his original capture, the Kzinti had considered him a vitally important prize, probably a Rimworld spy. Stockton and his tough crew reject this idea outright and seem to mistrust Locklear, who goes aboard the warship only under Stockton's orders. The ship sits in a clearing within sight of Locklear's little hut.

Lieutenant Grace Agostinho, the *Wayne*'s other officer, is a voluptuous eyeful who sees to Locklear's first civilized meal in months and befriends him aboard the cruiser. Under unofficial arrest, he is shown to a vacant crew cubicle for the night. Something is wrong about his impressions on that ship, but Locklear falls asleep unable to identify it.

He wakes in a cold sweat. *Everydamnthing* is wrong! The sloppy discipline; a tiny crew of thugs instead of a sharp combat team; the open drinking on duty watches; the dirty ship. Locklear sneaks from his cubicle long enough to verify his worst fears: the *Anthony Wayne* was a prisoner ship, and bloodstains suggest it has been taken over in a prisoner mutiny. This crew of renegades is hell-bent on finding a military secret that doesn't exist, and Locklear knows his life isn't worth spit. He manages to get back to sleep only by reminding himself that these bloody pirates don't know he's figured them out. . . .

PART TWO

Locklear awoke with a sensation of dread, then a brief upsurge of joy at sleeping in modern accomodations, and then he remembered his conclusions in the middle of the night, and his optimism fell off and broke.

To mend it, he decided to smile with the innocence of a Candide and plan his tactics. If he could get to the Kzin lifeboat, he might steer it like a slow battering ram and disable the *Anthony Wayne*. Or they might blow him to flinders in midair—and what if his fears were wrong, and despite all evidence this combat team was genuine? In any case, disabling the ship meant marooning the whole lot of them together. It wasn't a plan calculated to lengthen his life expectancy; maybe he would think of another.

The crew was already bustling around with breakfasts when he emerged, and yes, he could use the ship's cleaning unit for his clothes. When he asked for spare clothing, Soichiro Lee was first to deny it to him. "Our spares are still—contaminated from a previous engagement," he explained, with a meaningful look toward Gomulka.

I bet they are, with blood, Locklear told himself as he scooped his synthesized eggs and bacon. Their uniforms all seemed to fit well. Probably their own, he decided. The stylized winged gun on Gomulka's patch said he could fly gunships. Lee might be a medic, and the sensuous Grace might be a real intelligence officer—and all could be renegades.

Stockton watched him eat, friendly as ever, arms folded and relaxed. "Gomulka and Gazho did a recon in our pinnace at dawn," he said, sucking a tooth. "Seems your apemen are already rebuilding at another site; a terrace at this end of the lake. A lot closer to us."

"I wish you could think of them as people," Locklear said. "They're not terribly bright, but they don't swing on vines."

Chuckling: "Bright enough to be nuisances, perhaps try and burn us out if they find the ship here," Stockton said. "Maybe bright enough to know what it is the tabbies found here. You said they can talk a little. Well, you can help us interrogate 'em."

"They aren't too happy with me," Locklear admitted as Gomulka sat down with steaming coffee. "But I'll try on one condition."

Gomulka's voice carried a rumble of barely hidden threat. "Conditions? You're talking to your commander, Locklear."

"It's a very simple one," Locklear said softly. "No more killing or threatening these people. They call themselves 'gentles,' and they are. The New Smithson, or half the Interworld University branches, would give a year's budget to study them alive."

Grace Agostinho had been working at a map terminal, but evidently with an ear open to their negotiations. As Stockton and Gomulka gazed at each other in silent surmise, she took the few steps to sit beside Locklear, her hip warm against his. "You're an ethologist. Tell me, what could the Kzinti do with these gentles?"

Locklear nodded, sipped coffee, and finally said, "I'm not sure. Study them hoping for insights into the underlying psychology of modern humans, maybe."

Stockton said, "But you said the tabbies don't know about them."

"True; at least I don't see how they could. But you asked, I can't believe the gentles would know what you're after, but if you have to ask them, of course I'll help."

Stockton said it was necessary, and appointed Lee acting corporal at the cabin as he filled most of the pinnace's jumpseats with himself, Locklear, Agostinho, Gomulka, and the lank Parker. The little craft sat on downsloping delta wings that ordinarily nested against the *Wayne*'s hull, and had intakes for gas-reactor jets. "Newest piece of hardware we have," Stockton said, patting the pilot's console. It was Gomulka, however, who took the controls.

Locklear suggested that they approach very slowly, with hands visibly up and empty, as they settled the pinnace near the beginnings of a new gentles campsite.

The gentles, including their women, all rushed for primitive lances but did not flee, and Anse Parker was the only one carrying an obvious weapon as the pinnace's canopy swung back. Locklear stepped forward, talking and smiling, with Parker at their backs. He saw Ruth waiting for old Gimp, and said he was much happy to see her, which was an understatement. Minuteman, too, had survived the firing on their village.

Cloud had not. Ruth told him so immediately. "Locklear make many deaths to gentles," she accused. Behind her, some of the gentles stared with faces that were anything but gentle. "Gentles not like talk to Locklear, he says. Go now. Please," she added, one of the last words he'd taught her, and she said it with urgency. Her glance toward Grace Agostinho was interested, not hostile but perhaps pitying.

Locklear moved away from the others, farther from the glaring Gimp. "More new people come," he called from a distance, pleading. "Think gentles big, bad animals. Stop when they see gentles; much much sorry. Locklear say not hurt gentles more."

With her head cocked sideways, Ruth seemed to be testing his mind for lies. She spoke with Gimp, whose face registered a deep sadness and, perhaps, some confusion as well. Locklear could hear a buzz of low conversation between Stockton nearby and Gomulka, who still sat at the pinnace controls.

"Locklear think good, but bad things happen," Ruth said at last. "Kill Cloud, many more. Gentles not like fight. Locklear know this," she said, almost crying now. "Please go!"

Gomulka came out of the pinnace with his sidearm drawn, and Locklear turned toward him, aghast. "No shooting! You promised," he reminded Stockton.

But: "We'll have to bring the ape-woman with the old man," Stockton said grimly, not liking it but determined. Gomulka stood quietly, the big sloping shoulders hunched.

Stockton said, "This is an explosive situation, Locklear. We must take those two for interrogation. Have the woman tell them we won't hurt them unless their people try to hunt us."

Then, as Locklear froze in horrified anger, Gomulka bellowed, *"Tell 'em!"*

Locklear did it and Ruth began to call in their language to the assembled throng. Then, at Gomulka's command, Parker ran forward to grasp the pathetic old Gimp by the arm, standing more than a head taller than the Neanderthal. That was the moment when Minuteman, who must have understood only a little of their parley, leaped weaponless at the big belter.

Parker swept a contemptuous arm at the little fellow's reach, but let out a howl as Minuteman, with those blacksmith arms of his, wrenched that arm as one would wave a stick.

The report was shattering, with echoes slapping off the lake, and Locklear whirled to see Gomulka's two-handed aim with the projectile sidearm. "No! Goddammit, these are human beings," he screamed, rushing toward the fallen Minuteman, falling on his knees, placing one hand over the little fellow's breast as if to stop the blood that was pumping from it. The gentles panicked at the thunder from Gomulka's weapons, and began to run.

Minuteman's throat pulse still throbbed, but he was in deep shock from the heavy projectile and his pulse died as Locklear watched helpless. Parker was already clubbing old Gimp with his rifle-butt and Gomulka, his sidearm out of sight, grabbed Ruth as she tried to interfere. The big man might as well have walked into a train wreck while the train was still moving.

Grace Agostinho seemed to know she was no fighter, retreating into the pinnace. Stockton, whipping the ornamental braid from his epaulets, began to fashion nooses as he moved to help Parker, whose left arm was half-useless. Locklear came to his feet, saw Gomulka's big fist smash at Ruth's temple, and dived into the fray with one arm locked around Gomulka's bull neck, trying to haul him off-balance. Both of Ruth's hands grappled with Gomulka's now, and Locklear saw that she was slowly overpowering him while her big teeth sought his throat, only the whites of her eyes showing. It was the last thing Locklear would see for awhile, as someone raced up behind him.

He awoke to a gentle touch and the chill of antiseptic spray behind his right ear, and focused on the real concern mirrored on Stockton's face. He lay in the room he had built for Loli, Soichiro Lee kneeling beside him, while Ruth and Gimp huddled as far as they could get into a corner. Stockton held a standard issue parabellum, arms folded, not pointing the weapon but keeping it in evidence. "Only a mild concussion," Lee murmured to the commander.

"You with us again, Locklear?" Stockton got a nod in response, motioned for Lee to leave, and sighed. "I'm truly sorry about all this, but you were interfering with a military operation. Gomulka is—he has a lot of experience, and a good commander would be stupid to ignore his suggestions."

Locklear was barely wise enough to avoid saying that Gomulka did more commanding than Stockton did. Pushing himself up, blinking from the headache that split his skull like an axe, he said, "I need some air."

"You'll have to get it right here," Stockton said, "because I can't—won't let you out. Consider yourself under arrest. Behave yourself and that could change." With that, he shouldered the woven mat aside and his slow footsteps echoed down the connecting corridor to the other room.

Without a door directly to the outside, he would have to run down that corridor where armed yahoos waited. Digging out would make noise and might take hours. Locklear slid down against the cabin wall, head in hands. When he opened them again he saw that poor old Gimp seemed comatose, but Ruth was looking at him intently. "I wanted to be friend of all gentles," he sighed.

"Yes. Gentles know," she replied softly. "New people with gentles not good. Stok-Tun not want hurt, but others not care about gentles. Ruth hear in head," she added, with a palm against the top of her head.

"Ruth must not tell," Locklear insisted. "New people maybe kill if they know gentles hear that way."

She gave him a very modern nod, and even in that hopelessly homely face, her shy smile held a certain beauty. "Locklear help Ruth fight. Ruth like Locklear much, much; even if Locklear is—new."

"Ruth, 'new' means 'ugly,' doesn't it? New, new," he repeated, screwing his face into a hideous caricature, making claws of his hands, snarling in exaggerated mimicry.

He heard voices raised in muffled excitement in the other room, and Ruth's head was cocked again momentarily. "Ugly?" She made faces, too. "Part yes. New means not same as before but also ugly, maybe bad."

"All the gentles considered me the ugly man. Yes?"

"Yes," she replied sadly. "Ruth not care. Like ugly man if good man, too."

"And you knew I thought you were, uh . . ."

"Ugly? Yes. Ruth try and fix before."

"I know," he said, miserable. "Locklear like Ruth for that and many, many more things."

Quickly, as boots stamped in the corridor, she said, "Big problem. New people not think Locklear tell truth. New woman—"

Schmidt's rifle barrel moved the mat aside and he let it do his gesturing to Locklear. "On your feet, buddy, you've got some explaining to do."

Locklear got up carefully so his head would not roll off his shoulders. Stumbling toward the doorway he said to Ruth: "What about new woman?"

"Much, much new in head. Ruth feel sorry," she called as Locklear moved toward the other room.

They were all crowded in, and seven pairs of eyes were intent on Locklear. Grace's gaze held a liquid warmth but he saw nothing warmer than icicles in any other face. Gomulka and Stockton sat on the benches facing him across his crude table like judges at a trial. Locklear did not have to be told to stand before them.

Gomulka reached down at his own feet and grunted with effort, and the toolbox crashed down on the table.

His voice was not its usual command timbre, but menacingly soft. "Gazho noticed this was all tabby stuff," he said.

"Part of an honorable trade," Locklear said, drymouthed. "I could have killed a Kzin and didn't."

"They trade you a fucking LIFEBOAT, too?"

Those goddamn pinnace sorties of his! The light of righteous fury snapped in the big man's face, but Locklear stared back. "Matter of fact, yes. The Kzin is a cat of his word, sergeant."

"Enough of your bullshit, I want the truth!"

Now Locklear shifted his gaze to Stockton. "I'm telling it. Enough of your bullshit, too. How did your bunch of bozos get out of the brig, Stockton?"

Parker blurted, "How the hell did—" before Gomulka spun on his bench with a silent glare. Parker blushed and swallowed.

"We're asking the questions, Locklear. The tabbies must've left you a girlfriend, too," Stockton said quietly. "Lee and Schmidt both saw some little hotsy queen of the jungle out near the perimeter while we were gone. Make no mistake, they'll hunt her down and there's nothing I can say to stop them."

"Why not, if you're a commander?"

Stockton flushed angrily, with a glance at Gomulka that was not kind. "That's my problem, not yours. Look, you want some straight talk, and here it is: Agostinho has seen the goddamned translations from a tabby dreadnaught, and there *is* something on this godforsaken place they think is important, and we were in this Rim sector when—when we got into some problems, and she told me. I'm an officer, I really am, believe what you like. But we have to find whatever the hell there is on Zoo."

"So you can plea-bargain after your mutiny?"

"That's ENOUGH," Gomulka bellowed. "You're a little too cute for your own good, Locklear. But if you're ever gonna get off this ball of dirt, it'll be after you help us find what the tabbies are after."

"It's me," Locklear said simply. "I've already told you."

Silent consternation, followed by disbelief. "And what the fuck are you," Gomulka spat.

"Not much, I admit. But as I told you, they captured me and got the idea I knew more about the Rim sectors than I do."

"How much Kzinshit do you think I'll swallow?" Gomulka was standing, now, advancing around the table toward his captive. Curt Stockton shut his eyes and sighed his helplessness.

Locklear was wondering if he could grab anything from the toolbox when a voice of sweet reason stopped Gomulka. "Brutality hasn't solved anything here yet," said Grace Agostinho. "I'd like to talk to Locklear alone." Gomulka stopped, glared at her, then back at Locklear. "I can't do any worse than you have, David," she added to the fuming sergeant.

Beckoning, she walked to the doorway and Gazho made sure his rifle muzzle grated on Locklear's ribs as the ethologist followed her outside. She said, "Do I have your honorable parole? Bear in mind that even if you try to run, they'll soon have you and the girl who's running loose, too. They've already destroyed some kind of flying raft; yours, I take it," she smiled.

Damn, hell, shit, and blast! "Mine. I won't run, Grace. Besides, you've got a parabellum."

"Remember that," she said, and began to stroll toward the trees while the cabin erupted with argument. Locklear vented more silent damns and hells; she wasn't leading him anywhere near his hidden Kzin sidearm.

Grace Agostinho, surprisingly, first asked about Loli. She seemed amused to learn he had waked the girl first, and that he'd regretted it at his leisure. Gradually, her questions segued to answers. "Discipline on a warship can be vicious," she mused as if to herself. "Curt Stockton was—is a career officer, but it's his view that there must be limits to discipline. His own commander was a hard man, and—"

"Jesus Christ; you're saying he mutinied like Fletcher Christian?"

"That's not entirely wrong," she said, now very feminine as they moved into a glade, out of sight of the cabin. "David Gomulka is a rougher sort, a man of some limited ideas but more of action. I'm afraid Curt filled David with ideas that, ah, . . ."

"Stockton started a boulder downhill and can't stop it," Locklear said. "Not the first time a man of ideas has started something he can't control. How'd you get into this mess?"

"An affair of the heart; I'd rather not talk about it. When I'm drawn to a man, . . . well, I tend to show it," she said, and preened her hair for him as she leaned against a fallen tree. "You must tell them what they want to know, my dear. These are desperate men, in desperate trouble."

Locklear saw the promise in those huge dark eyes and gazed into them. "I swear to you, the Kzinti thought I was some kind of Interworld agent, but they dropped me on Zoo for safekeeping."

"And were you?" Softly, softly, catchee monkey . . .

"Good God, no! I'm an—"

"Ethologist. I heard it. But the Kzin suspicion does seem reasonable, doesn't it?"

"I guess, if you're paranoid." *God, but this is one seductive lieutenant.*

"Which means that David and Curt could sell you to the Kzinti for safe passage, if I let them," she said, moving toward him, her hands pulling apart the closures on his flight suit. "But I don't think that's the secret, and I don't think *you* think so. You're a fascinating man, and I don't know when I've been so attracted to anyone. Is this so awful of me?"

He knew damned well how powerfully persuasive a woman like Grace could be with that voluptuous willowy sexuality of hers. And he remembered Ruth's warning, and believed it. But he would rather drown in honey than in vinegar, and when she turned her face upward, he found her mouth with his, and willingly let her lust kindle his own.

Presently, lying on forest humus and watching Grace comb her hair clean with her fingers, Locklear's breathing slowed. He inventoried her charms as she shrugged into her flight suit again; returned her impudent smile;

began to readjust his togs. "If this be torture," he declaimed like an actor, "make the most of it."

"Up to the standards of your local ladies?"

"Oh yes," he said fervently, knowing it was only a small lie. "But I'm not sure I understand why you offered."

She squatted becomingly on her knees, brushing at his clothing. "You're very attractive," she said. "And mysterious. And if you'll help us, Locklear, I promise to plumb your mysteries as much as you like—and vice-versa."

"An offer I can't refuse, Grace. But I don't know how I can do more than I have already."

Her frown held little anger; more of perplexity. "But I've told you, my dear: we must have that Kzin secret."

"And you didn't believe what I said."

Her secret smile again, teasing: "Really, darling, you must give me some credit. I *am* in the intelligence corps."

He did see a flash of irritation cross her face this time as he laughed. "Grace, this is crazy," he said, still grinning. "It may be absurd that the Kzinti thought I was an agent, but it's true. I think the planet itself is a mind-boggling discovery, and I said so first thing off. Other than that, what can I say?"

"I'm sorry you're going to be this way about it," she said with the pout of a nubile teen-ager, then hitched up the sidearm on her belt as if to remind him of it.

She's sure something, he thought as they strode back to his clearing. *If I had any secret to hide, could she get it out of me with this kind of attention? Maybe—but she's all technique and no real passion. Exactly the girl you want to bring home to your friendly regimental combat team . . .*

Grace motioned him into the cabin without a word and, as Schmidt sent him into the room with Ruth and the old man, he saw both Gomulka and Stockton leave the cabin with Grace. *I don't think she has affairs of the heart*, he reflected with a wry smile. *Affairs of the glands beyond counting, but maybe no heart to lose. Or no character?*

He sat down near Ruth, who was sitting with Gimp's head in her lap, and sighed. "Ruth much smart about new woman. Locklear see now," he said and, gently, kissed the homely face.

The crew had a late lunch but brought none for their captives, and Locklear was taken to his judges in the afternoon. He saw hammocks slung in his room, evidence that the crew intended to stay awhile. Stockton, as usual, began as pleasantly as he could. "Locklear, since you're not on Agostinho's list of known intelligence assets in the Rim sectors, then maybe we've been peering at the wrong side of the coin."

"That's what I told the tabbies," Locklear said.

"Now we're getting somewhere. Actually, you're a Kzin agent; right?"

Locklear stared, then tried not to laugh. "Oh, Jesus, Stockton! Why would they drop me here, in that case?"

Evidently, Stockton's pleasant side was loosely attached under trying circumstances. He flushed angrily. "You tell us."

"You can find out damned fast by turning me over to Interworld authorities," Locklear reminded him.

"And if you turn out to be a plugged nickel," Gomulka snarled, "you're home free and we're in deep shit. No, I don't think we will, little man. We'll do anything we have to do to get the facts out of you. If it takes shooting hostages, we will."

Locklear switched his gaze to the bedeviled Stockton and saw no help there. At this point, a few lies might help the gentles. "A real officer, are you? Shoot these poor savages? Go ahead, actually you might be doing me a favor. You can see they hate my guts! The only reason they didn't kill me today is that they think I'm one of you, and they're scared to. Every one you knock off, or chase off, is just one less who's out to tan my hide."

Gomulka, slyly: "So how'd you say you got that tabby ship?"

Locklear: "On Kzersatz. Call it grand theft, I don't give a damn." Knowing they would explore Kzersatz sooner or later, he said, "The tabbies probably thought I hightailed it for the Interworld fleet but I could barely fly the thing. I was lucky to get down here in one piece."

Stockton's chin jerked up. "Do you mean there's a Kzin force right across those force walls?"

"There was; I took care of them myself."

Gomulka stood up now. "Sure you did. I never heard such jizm in twenty years of barracks brags. Grace, you never did like a lot of hollering and blood. Go to the ship." Without a word, and with the same liquid gaze she would turn on Locklear—and perhaps on anyone else—she nodded and walked out.

As Gomulka reached for his captive, Locklear grabbed for the heavy toolbox. That little hand welder would ruin a man's entire afternoon. Gomulka nodded, and suddenly Locklear felt his arms gripped from behind by Schmidt's big hands. He brought both feet up, kicked hard against the table, and as the table flew into the faces of Stockton and Gomulka, Schmidt found himself propelled backward against the cabin wall.

Shouting, cursing, they overpowered Locklear at last, hauling the top of his flight suit down so that its arms could be tied into a sort of straitjacket. Breathing hard, Gomulka issued his final backhand slap toward Locklear's mouth. Locklear ducked, then spat into the big man's face.

Wiping spittle away with his sleeve, Gomulka muttered, "Curt, we gotta soften this guy up."

Stockton pointed to the scars on Locklear's upper body. "You know, I don't think he softens very well, David. Ask yourself whether you think it's useful, or whether you just want to do it."

It was another of those ideas Gomulka seemed to value greatly because he had so few of his own. "Well goddammit, what would you do?"

"Coercion may work, but not this kind." Studying the silent Locklear in the grip of three men, he came near smiling. "Maybe give him a comm set and drop him among the Neanderthals. When he's good and ready to talk, we rescue him."

A murmur among the men, and a snicker from Gazho. To prove he did have occasional ideas, Gomulka replied, "Maybe. Or better, maybe drop him next door on Kzinkatz or whatever the fuck he calls it." His eyes slid slowly to Locklear.

To Locklear, who was licking a trickle of blood from his upper lip, the suggestion did not register for a count of two beats. When it did, he needed a third beat to make the right response. Eyes wide, he screamed.

"Yeah," said Nathan Gazho.

"Yeah, right," came the chorus.

Locklear struggled, but not too hard. "My God! They'll— They EAT people, Stockton!"

"Well, it looks like a voice vote, Curt," Gomulka drawled, very pleased with his idea, then turned to Locklear. "But that's democracy for you. You'll have a nice comm set and you can call us when you're ready. Just don't forget the story about the boy who cried 'wolf.' But when you call, Locklear—" the big sergeant's voice was low and almost pleasant, "—be ready to deal."

Locklear felt a wild impulse, as Gomulka shoved him into the pinnace, to beg, "Please, Bre'r Fox, don't throw me in the briar patch!" He thrashed a bit and let his eyes roll convincingly until Parker, with a choke hold, pacified him half-unconscious.

If he had any doubts that the pinnace was orbit-rated, Locklear lost them as he watched Gomulka at work. Parker sat with the captive though Lee, beside Gomulka, faced a console. The three pirates negotiated a three-way bet on how much time would pass before Locklear begged to be picked up. His comm set, roughly shoved into his ear with its button switch, had fresh batteries but Lee reminded him again that they would be returning only once to bail him out. The pinnace, a lovely little craft, arced up to orbital height and, with only its transparent canopy between him and hard vac, Locklear found real fear added to his pretense. After pitchover, tiny bursts of light at the wingtips steadied the pinnace as it began its re-entry over the saffron jungles of Kzersatz.

Because of its different schedule, the tiny programmed sunlet of Kzersatz was only an hour into its morning. "Keep one eye on your sweep screen," Gomulka said as the roar of deceleration died away.

"I am," Lee replied grimly. "Locklear, if we get jumped by a tabby ship I'll put a burst right into your guts, first thing."

As Locklear made a show of moaning and straining at his bonds, Gomulka banked the pinnace for its mapping sweep. Presently, Lee's infrared scanners flashed an overlay on his screen and Gomulka nodded, but finished the sweep. Then, by manual control, he slowed the little craft and brought it at a leisurely pace to the I R blips, a mile or so above the alien veldt. Lee brought the screen's video to high magnification.

Anse Parker saw what Locklear saw. "Only a few tabbies, huh? And you took care of 'em, huh? You son of a bitch!" He glared at the scene, where a dozen Kzinti moved unaware amid half-submerged huts and cooking fires, and swatted Locklear across the back of his head with an open hand. "Looks like they've gone native," Parker went on. "Hey, Gomulka: they'll be candy for us."

"I noticed," Gomulka replied. "You know what? If we bag 'cm now, we're helping this little shit. We can come back any time we like, maybe have ourselves a tabby-hunt."

"Yeah; show 'em what it's like," Lee snickered, "after they've had their manhunt."

Locklear groaned for effect. *A village ready-made in only a few months! Scarface didn't waste any time getting his own primitives out of stasis. I hope to God he doesn't show up looking glad to see me.* To avoid that possibility he pleaded, "Aren't you going to give me a running chance?"

"Sure we are," Gomulka laughed. "Tabbies will pick up your scent anyway. Be on you like flies on a turd." The pinnace flew on, unseen from far below, Lee bringing up the video now and then. Once he said, "Can't figure out what they're hunting in that field. If I didn't know Kzinti were strict carnivores I'd say they were farming."

Locklear knew that primitive Kzinti ate vegetables as well, and so did their meat animals; but he kept his silence. It hadn't even occurred to these piratical deserters that the Kzinti below might be as prehistoric as Neanderthalers. Good; let them think they understood the Kzinti! *But nobody knows 'em like I do*, he thought. It was an arrogance he would recall with bitterness very, very soon.

Gomulka set the pinnace down with practiced ease behind a stone escarpment and Parker, his gaze nervously sweeping the jungle, used his gunbarrel to urge Locklear out of the craft.

Soichiro Lee's gentle smile did not match his final words: "If you manage to hide out here, just remember we'll pick up your little girlfriend before long. Probably a better piece of snatch than the Manaus machine," he went on, despite a sudden glare from Gomulka. "How long do you want us to use her, asshole? Think about it," he winked, and the canopy's "thunk" muffled the guffaws of Anse Parker.

Locklear raced away as the pinnace lifted, making it look good. They had tossed Bre'r Rabbit into his personal briar patch, never suspecting he might have friends here.

He was thankful that the village lay downhill as he began his one athletic specialty, long-distance jogging, because he could once again feel the synthetic gravity of Kzersatz tugging at his body. He judged that he was a two-hour trot from the village and paced himself carefully, walking and resting now and then. And planning.

As soon as Scarface learned the facts, they could set a trap for the returning pinnace. And then, with captives of his own, Locklear could negotiate with Stockton. It was clear by now that Curt Stockton considered himself a leader of virtue—because he was a man of ideas. David Gomulka was a man of action without many

important ideas, the perfect model of a playground
bully long after graduation.

And Stockton? He would've been the kind of clever
kid who decided early that violence was an inferior way
to do things, because he wasn't very good at it himself.
Instead, he'd enlist a Gomulka to stand nearby while
the clever kid tried to beat you up with words; debate
you to death. And if that finally failed, he could always
sigh, and walk away leaving the bully to do his dirty
work, and imagine that his own hands were clean.

But Kzersatz was a whole 'nother playground, with
different rules. Locklear smiled at the thought and jogged
on.

An hour later he heard the beast crashing in panic
through orange ferns before he saw it, and realized that
it was pursued only when he spied a young male flashing with sinuous efficiency behind.

No one ever made friends with a Kzin by interrupt-
ing its hunt, so Locklear stood motionless among
palmferns and watched. The prey reminded him of a
pygmy tyrannosaur, almost the height of a man but
with teeth meant for grazing on foliage. The Kzin
bounded nearer, disdaining the *wtsai* knife at his belt,
and screamed only as he leaped for the kill.

The prey's armored hide and thrashing tail made the
struggle interesting, but the issue was never in doubt.
A Kzin warrior was trained to hunt, to kill, and to eat
that kill, from kittenhood. The roars of the lizard dwin-
dled to a hissing gurgle; the tail and the powerful legs
stilled. Only after the Kzin vented his victory scream
and ripped into his prey did Locklear step into the
clearing made by flattened ferns.

Hands up and empty, Locklear called in Kzin, "The
Kzin is a mighty hunter!" To speak in Kzin, one needed
a good falsetto and plenty of spit. Locklear's command
was fair, but the young Kzin reacted as though the man
had spouted fire and brimstone. He paused only long
enough to snatch up his kill, a good hundred kilos,
before bounding off at top speed.

Crestfallen, Locklear trotted toward the village again.
He wondered now if Scarface and Kit, the mate Locklear

had freed for him, had failed to speak of mankind to the ancient Kzin tribe. In any case, they would surely respond to his use of their language until he could get Scarface's help. Perhaps the young male had simply raced away to bring the good news.

And perhaps, he decided a half-hour later, he himself was the biggest fool in Known Space or beyond it. They had ringed him before he knew it, padding silently through foliage the same mottled yellows and oranges as their fur. Then, almost simultaneously, he saw several great tigerish shapes disengage from their camouflage ahead of him, and heard the scream as one leapt upon him from behind.

Bowled over by the rush, feeling hot breath and fangs at his throat, Locklear moved only his eyes. His attacker might have been the same one he surprised while hunting, and he felt needle-tipped claws through his flight suit.

Then Locklear did the only things he could: kept his temper, swallowed his terror, and repeated his first greeting: "The Kzin is a mighty hunter."

He saw, striding forward, an old Kzin with ornate bandolier straps. The oldster called to the others, "It is true, the beast speaks the Hero's Tongue! It is as I prophesied." Then, to the young attacker, "Stand away at the ready," and Locklear felt like breathing again.

"I am Locklear, who first waked members of your clan from age-long sleep," he said in that ancient dialect he'd learned from Kit. "I come in friendship. May I rise?"

A contemptuous gesture and, as Locklear stood up, a worse remark. "Then you are the beast that lay with a palace *prret*, a courtesan. We have heard. You will win no friends here."

A cold tendril marched down Locklear's spine. "May I speak with my friends? The Kzinti have things to fear, but I am not among them."

More laughter. "The Rockear beast thinks it is fearsome," said the young male, his ear-umbrellas twitching in merriment.

"I come to ask help, and to offer it," Locklear said evenly.

"The priesthood knows enough of your help. Come," said the older one. And that is how Locklear was marched into a village of prehistoric Kzinti, ringed by hostile predators twice his size.

His reception party was all-male, its members staring at him in frank curiosity while prodding him to the village. They finally left him in an open area surrounded by huts with his hands tied, a leather collar around his neck, the collar linked by a short braided rope to a hefty stake. When he squatted on the turf, he noticed the soil was torn by hooves here and there. Dark stains and an abbatoir odor said the place was used for butchering animals. The curious gazes of passing females said he was only a strange animal to them. The disappearance of the males into the largest of the semi-submerged huts suggested that he had furnished the village with something worth a town meeting.

At last the meeting broke up, Kzin males striding from the hut toward him, a half-dozen of the oldest emerging last, each with a four-fingered paw tucked into his bandolier belt. Prominent scars across the breasts of these few were all exactly similar; some kind of self-torture ritual, Locklear guessed. Last of all with the ritual scars was the old one he'd spoken with, and this one had *both* paws tucked into his belt. *Got it; the higher your status, the less you need to keep your hands ready, or to hurry.*

The old devil was enjoying all this ceremony, and so were the other big shots. Standing in clearly-separated rings behind them were the other males with a few females, then the other females, evidently the entire tribe. Locklear spotted a few Kzinti whose expressions and ear-umbrellas said they were either sick or unhappy, but all played their obedient parts.

Standing before him, the oldster reached out and raked Locklear's face with what seemed to be only a ceremonial insult. It brought welts to his cheek anyway. The oldster spoke for all to hear. "You began the tribe's awakening, and for that we promise a quick kill."

"I waked several Kzinti, who promised me honor," Locklear managed to say.

"Traitors? They have no friends here. So *you*—have no friends here," said the old Kzin with pompous dignity. "This the priesthood has decided."

"You are the leader?"

"First among equals," said the high priest with a smirk that said he believed in no equals.

"While this tribe slept," Locklear said loudly, hoping to gain some support, "a mighty Kzin warrior came here. I call him Scarface. I return in peace to see him, and to warn you that others who look like me may soon return. They wish you harm, but I do not. Would you take me to Scarface?"

He could not decipher the murmurs, but he knew amusement when he saw it. The high priest stepped forward, untied the rope, handed it to the nearest of the husky males who stood behind the priests. "He would see the mighty hunter who had new ideas," he said. "Take him to see that hero, so that he will fully appreciate the situation. Then bring him back to the ceremony post."

With that, the high priest turned his back and followed by the other priests, walked away. The dozens of other Kzinti hurried off, carefully avoiding any backward glances. Locklear said, to the huge specimen tugging on his neck rope, "I cannot walk quickly with hands behind my back."

"Then you must learn," rumbled the big Kzin, and lashed out with a foot that propelled Locklear forward. *I think he pulled that punch*, Locklear thought. *Kept his claws retracted, at least.* The Kzin led him silently from the village and along a path until hidden by foliage. Then, "You are the Rockear," he said, slowing. "I am (something as unpronounceable as most Kzin names)," he added, neither friendly nor unfriendly. He began untying Locklear's hands with, "I must kill you if you run, and I will. But I am no priest," he said, as if that explained his willingness to ease a captive's walking.

"You are a stalwart," Locklear said. "May I call you that?"

"As long as you can," the big Kzin said, leading the way again. "I voted to my priest to let you live, and teach us. So did most heroes of my group."

Uh-huh; they have priests instead of senators. But this smells like the old American system before direct elections. "Your priest is not bound to vote as you say?" A derisive snort was his answer, and he persisted. "Do you vote your priests in?"

"Yes. For life," said Stalwart, explaining everything.

"So they pretend to listen, but they do as they like," Locklear said.

A grunt, perhaps of admission or of scorn. "It was always thus," said Stalwart, and found that Locklear could trot, now. Another half-hour found them moving across a broad veldt, and Locklear saw the scars of a grass fire before he realized he was in familiar surroundings. Stalwart led the way to a rise and then stopped, pointing toward the jungle. "There," he said, "is your scarfaced friend."

Locklear looked in vain, then back at Stalwart. "He must be blending in with the ferns. You people do that very—"

"The highest tree. What remains of him is there."

And then Locklear saw the flying creatures he had called "batowls," tiny mites at a distance of two hundred meters, picking at tatters of something that hung in a net from the highest tree in the region. "Oh, my God! Won't he die there?"

"He is dead already. He underwent the long ceremony," said Stalwart, "many days past, with wounds that killed slowly."

Locklear's glare was incriminating: "I suppose you voted against that, too?"

"That, and the sacrifice of the palace *prret* in days past," said the Kzin.

Blinking away tears, for Scarface had truly been a cat of his word, Locklear said, "Those *prret*. One of them was Scarface's mate when I left. Is she—up there, too?"

For what it was worth, the big Kzin could not meet

his gaze. "Drowning is the dishonorable punishment for females," he said, pointing back toward Kzersatz's long shallow lake. "The priesthood never avoids tradition, and she lies beneath the water. Another *prret* with kittens was permitted to rejoin the tribe. She chose to be shunned instead. Now and then, we see her. It is treason to speak against the priesthood, and I will not."

Locklear squeezed his eyes shut; blinked; turned away from the hideous sight hanging from that distant tree as scavengers picked at its bones. "And I hoped to help your tribe! A pox on all your houses," he said to no one in particular. He did not speak to the Kzin again, but they did not hurry as Stalwart led the way back to the village.

The only speaking Locklear did was to the comm set in his ear, shoving its pushbutton switch. The Kzin looked back at him in curiosity once or twice, but now he was speaking Interworld, and perhaps Stalwart thought he was singing a death song.

In a way, it was true—though not a song of his own death, if he could help it. "Locklear calling the *Anthony Wayne*," he said, and paused.

He heard the voice of Grace Agostinho reply, "Recording."

"They've caught me already, and they intend to kill me. I don't much like you bastards, but at least you're human. I don't care how many of the male tabbies you bag; when they start torturing me I won't be any further use to you."

Again, Grace's voice replied in his ear: "Recording."

Now with a terrible suspicion, Locklear said, "Is anybody there? If you're monitoring me live, say 'monitoring.'"

His comm set, in Grace's voice, only said, "Recording."

Locklear flicked off the switch and began to walk even more slowly, until Stalwart tugged hard on the leash. Any Kzin who cared to look, as they re-entered the village, would have seen a little man bereft of hope. He did not complain when Stalwart retied his hands, nor even when another Kzin marched him away and fairly flung him into a tiny hut near the edge of the village. Eventually they flung a bloody hunk of some recent kill into his hut, but it was raw and, with his hands tied behind him, he could not have held it to his mouth.

Nor could he toggle his comm set, assuming it would carry past the roof thatch. He had not said he would be in the village, and they would very likely kill him along with everybody else in the village when they came. *If* they came.

He felt as though he would drown in cold waves of despair. A vicious priesthood had killed his friends and, even if he escaped for a time, he would be hunted down by the galaxy's most pitiless hunters. And if his own kind rescued him, they might cheerfully beat him to death trying to learn a secret he had already divulged. And even the gentle Neanderthalers hated him, now.

Why not just give up? I don't know why, he admitted to himself, and began to search for something to help him fray the thongs at his wrists. He finally chose a rough-barked post, sitting down in front of it and staring toward the Kzin male whose lower legs he could see beneath the door matting.

He rubbed until his wrists were as raw as that meat lying in the dust before him. Then he rubbed until his muscles refused to continue, his arms cramping horribly. By that time it was dark, and he kept falling into an exhausted, fitful sleep, starting to scratch at his bonds every time a cramp woke him. The fifth time he awoke, it was to the sounds of scratching again. And a soft, distant call outside, which his guard answered just as softly. It took Locklear a moment to realize that those scratching noises were not being made by *him.*

The scratching became louder, filling him with a dread of the unknown in the utter blackness of the Kzersatz night. Then he heard a scrabble of clods tumbling to the earthen floor. Low, urgent, in the fitzrowr of a female Kzin: "Rockear, quickly! Help widen this hole!"

He wanted to shout, remembering Boots, the new

mother of two who had scorned her tribe; but he whispered hoarsely: "Boots?"

An even more familiar voice than that of Boots. "She is entertaining your guard. Hurry!"

"Kit! I can't, my hands are tied," he groaned. "Kit, they said you were drowned."

"Idiots," said the familiar voice, panting as she worked. A very faint glow preceded the indomitable Kit, who had a modern Kzin beltpac and used its glowlamp for brief moments. Without slowing her frantic pace, she said softly, "They built a walkway into the lake and—dropped me from it. But my mate, your friend Scarface, knew what they intended. He told me to breathe—many times just before I fell. With all the stones—weighting me down, I simply walked on the bottom, between the pilings—and untied the stones beneath the planks near shore. Idiots," she said again, grunting as her fearsome claws ripped away another chunk of Kzersatz soil. Then, "Poor Rockear," she said, seeing him writhe toward her.

In another minute, with the glowlamp doused, Locklear heard the growling curses of Kit's passage into the hut. She'd said females were good tunnelers, but not until now had he realized just how good. The nearest cover must be a good ten meters away . . . "Jesus, don't bite my hand, Kit," he begged, feeling her fangs and the heat of her breath against his savaged wrists. A moment later he felt a flash of white-hot pain through his shoulders as his hands came free. He'd been cramped up so long it hurt to move freely. "Well, by God it'll just have to hurt," he said aloud to himself, and flexed his arms, groaning.

"I suppose you must hold to my tail," she said. He felt the long, wondrously luxuriant tail whisk across his chest and because it was totally dark, did as she told him. Nothing short of true and abiding friendship, he knew, would provoke her into such manhandling of her glorious, her sensual, her fundamental tail.

They scrambled past mounds of soft dirt until Locklear felt cool night air on his face. "You may quit insulting my tail now," Kit growled. "We must wait inside this tunnel awhile. You take this: I do not use it well."

He felt the cold competence of the object in his hand and exulted as he recognized it as a modern Kzin sidearm. Crawling near with his face at her shoulder, he said, "How'd you know exactly where I was?"

"Your little long-talker, of course. We could hear you moaning and panting in there, and the magic tools of my mate located you."

But I didn't have it turned on. Ohhh-no; I didn't KNOW it was turned on! The goddamned thing is transmitting all the time . . . He decided to score one for Stockton's people, and dug the comm set from his ear. Still in the tunnel, it wouldn't transmit well until he moved outside. Crush it? Bury it? Instead, he snapped the magazine from the sidearm and, after removing its ammunition, found that the tiny comm set would fit inside. Completely enclosed by metal, the comm set would transmit no more until he chose.

He got all but three of the rounds back in the magazine, cursing every sound he made, and then moved next to Kit again. "They showed me what they did to Scarface. I can't tell you how sorry I am, Kit. He was my friend, and they will pay for it."

"Oh, yes, they will pay," she hissed softly. "Make no mistake, he is still your friend."

A thrill of energy raced from the base of his skull down his arms and legs. "You're telling me he's alive?"

As if to save her the trouble of a reply, a male Kzin called softly from no more than three paces away: "Milady; do we have him?"

"Yes," Kit replied.

"Scarface! Thank God you're—"

"Not now," said the one-time warship commander. "Follow quietly."

Having slept near Kit for many weeks, Locklear recognized her steam-kettle hiss as a sufferer's sigh. "I know your nose is hopeless at following a spoor, Rockear. But try not to pull me completely apart this time." Again he felt that long bushy tail pass across his breast, but this time he tried to grip it more gently as they sped off into the night.

Sitting deep in a cave with rough furniture and booby-trapped tunnels, Locklear wolfed stew under the light of a Kzin glowlamp. He had slightly scandalized Kit with a hug, then did the same to Boots as the young mother entered the cave without her kittens. The guard would never be trusted to guard anything again, said the towering Scarface, but that rescue tunnel was proof that a Kzin had helped. Now they'd be looking for Boots, thinking she had done more than lure a guard thirty meters away.

Locklear told his tale of success, failure, and capture by human pirates as he finished eating, then asked for an update of the Kzersatz problem. Kit, it turned out, had warned Scarface against taking the priests from stasis but one of the devout and not entirely bright males they woke had done the deed anyway.

Scarface, with his small hidden cache of modern equipment, had expected to lead; had he not been Tzak-Commander, once upon a time? The priests had seemed to agree—long enough to make sure they could coerce enough followers. It seemed, said Scarface, that ancient Kzin priests hadn't the slightest compunctions about lying, unlike modern Kzinti. He had tried repeatedly to call Locklear with his all-band comm set, without success. Depending on long custom, demanding that tradition take precedence over new ways, the priests had engineered the capture of Scarface and Kit in a hook-net, the kind of cruel device that tore at the victim's flesh at the slightest movement.

Villagers had spent days in building that walkway out over a shallowly sloping lake, a labor of loathing for Kzinti who hated to soak in water. Once it was extended to the point where the water was four meters deep, the rough-hewn dock made an obvious reminder of ceremonial murder to any female who might try, as Kit and Boots had done ages before, to liberate herself from the ritual prostitution of yore.

And then, as additional mental torture, they told

their bound captives what to expect, and made Scarface watch as Kit was thrown into the lake. Boots, watching in horror from afar, had then watched the torture and disposal of Scarface. She was amazed when Kit appeared at her birthing bower, having seen her disappear with great stones into deep water. The next day, Kit had killed a big ruminant, climbing that tree at night to recover her mate and placing half of her kill in the net.

"My medkit did the rest," Scarface said, pointing to ugly scar tissue at several places on his big torso. "These scum have never seen anyone recover from deep body punctures. Antibiotics can be magic, if you stretch a point."

Locklear mused silently on their predicament for long minutes. Then: "Boots, you can't afford to hang around near the village anymore. You'll have to hide your kittens and—"

"They have my kittens," said Boots, with a glitter of pure hate in her eyes. "They will be cared for as long as I do not disturb the villagers."

"Who told you that?"

"The high priest," she said, mewling pitifully as she saw the glance of doubt pass between Locklear and Scarface. The priests were accomplished liars.

"We'd best get them back soon," Locklear suggested. "Are you sure this cave is secure?"

Scarface took him halfway out one tunnel and, using the glowlamp, showed him a trap of horrifying simplicity. It was a grav polarizer unit from one of the biggest cages, buried just beneath the tunnel floor with a switch hidden to one side. If you reached to the side carefully and turned the switch off, that hidden grav unit wouldn't hurl you against the roof of the tunnel as you walked over it. If you didn't, it did. Simple. Terrible. "I like it," Locklear smiled. "Any more tricks I'd better know before I plaster myself over your ceiling?"

There were, and Scarface showed them to him. "But the least energy expended, the least noise and alarm to do the job, the best. Instead of polarizers, we might bury some stasis units outside, perhaps at the entrance to their meeting hut. Then we catch those *kshat* priests, and use the lying scum for target practice."

"Good idea, and we may be able to improve on it. How many units here in the cave?"

That was the problem; two stasis units taken from cages were not enough. They needed more from the crypt, said Locklear.

"They destroyed that little airboat you left me, but I built a better one," Scarface said with a flicker of humor from his ears.

"So did I. Put a bunch of polarizers on it to push yourself around and ignored the sail, didn't you?" He saw Scarface's assent and winked.

"Two units might work if we trap the priests one by one," Scarface hazarded. "But they've been meddling in the crypt. We might have to fight our way in. And you . . ." he hesitated.

"And I have fought better Kzinti before, and here I stand," Locklear said simply.

"That you do." They gripped hands, and then went back to set up their raid on the crypt. The night was almost done.

When surrendering, Scarface had told Locklear nothing of his equipment cache. With two sidearms he could have made life interesting for a man; interesting and short. But his word had been his bond, and now Locklear was damned glad to have the stuff.

They left the females to guard the cave. Flitting low across the veldt toward the stasis crypt with Scarface at his scooter controls, they planned their tactics. "I wonder why you didn't start shooting those priests the minute you were back on your feet," Locklear said over the whistle of breeze in their faces.

"The kittens," Scarface explained. "I might kill one or two priests before the cowards hid and sent innocent fools to be shot, but they are perfectly capable of hanging a kitten in the village until I gave myself up. And I did not dare raid the crypt for stasis units without a warrior to back me up."

"And I'll have to do," Locklear grinned.

"You will," Scarface grinned back; a typical Kzin grin, all business, no pleasure.

They settled the scooter near the ice-rimmed force wall and moved according to plan, making haste slowly to avoid the slightest sound, the huge Kzin's head swathed in a bandage of leaves that suggested a wound while—with luck—hiding his identity for a few crucial seconds.

Watching the Kzin warrior's muscular body slide among weeds and rocks, Locklear realized that Scarface was still not fully recovered from his ordeal. *He made his move before he was ready because of me, and I'm not even a Kzin. Wish I thought I could match that kind of commitment*, Locklear mused as he took his place in front of Scarface at the crypt entrance. His sidearm was in his hand. Scarface had sworn the priests had no idea what the weapon was and, with this kind of ploy, Locklear prayed he was right. Scarface gripped Locklear by the neck then, but gently, and they marched in together expecting to meet a guard just inside the entrance.

No guard. No sound at all—and then a distant hollow slam, as of a great box closing. They split up then, moving down each side corridor, returning to the main shaft silently, exploring side corridors again. After four of these forays, they knew that no one would be at their backs.

Locklear was peering into the fifth when, glancing back, he saw Scarface's gesture of caution. Scuffing steps down the side passage, a mumble in Kzin, then silence. Then Scarface resumed his hold on his friend's neck and, after one mutual glance of worry, shoved Locklear into the side passage.

"Ho, see the beast I captured," Scarface called, his voice booming in the wide passage, prompting exclamations from two surprised Kzin males.

Stasis cages lay in disarray, some open, some with transparent tops ripped off. One Kzin, with the breast scars and bandoliers of a priest, hopped off the cage he used as a seat, and placed a hand on the butt of his sharp *wtsai*. The other bore scabs on his breast and wore no bandolier. He had been tinkering with the innards of a small stasis cage, but whirled, jaw agape.

"It must have escaped after we left, yesterday," said

the priest, looking at the "captive," then with fresh curiosity at Scarface. "And who are—"

At that instant, Locklear saw what levitated, spinning, inside one of the medium-sized cages; spinning almost too fast to identify. But Locklear knew what it had to be, and while the priest was staring hard at Scarface, the little man lost control.

His cry was in Interworld, not Kzin: "You filthy bastard!" Before the priest could react, a roundhouse right with the massive barrel of a Kzin pistol took away both upper and lower incisors from the left side of his mouth. Caught this suddenly, even a two-hundred kilo Kzin could be sent reeling from the blow, and as the priest reeled to his right, Locklear kicked hard at his backside.

Scarface clubbed at the second Kzin, the corridor ringing with snarls and zaps of warrior rage. Locklear did not even notice, leaping on the back of the fallen priest, hacking with his gunbarrel until the *wtsai* flew from a smashed hand, kicking down with all his might against the back of the priest's head. The priest, at least twice Locklear's bulk, had lived a life much too soft, for far too long. He rolled over, eyes wide not in fear but in anger at this outrage from a puny beast. It is barely possible that fear might have worked.

The priest caught Locklear's boot in a mouthful of broken teeth, not seeing the sidearm as it swung at his temple. The thump was like an iron bar against a melon, the priest falling limp as suddenly as if some switch had been thrown.

Sobbing, Locklear dropped the pistol, grabbed handfuls of ear on each side, and pounded the priest's head against cruel obsidian until he felt a heavy grip on his shoulder.

"He is dead, Locklear. Save your strength," Scarface advised. As Locklear recovered his weapon and stumbled to his feet, he was shaking uncontrollably. "You must hate our kind more than I thought," Scarface added, studying Locklear oddly.

"He wasn't your kind. I would kill a man for the same crime," Locklear said in fury, glaring at the second Kzin who squatted, bloody-faced, in a corner holding a forearm with an extra elbow in it. Then Locklear rushed to open the cage the priest had been watching.

The top levered back, and its occupant sank to the cage floor without moving. Scarface screamed his rage, turning toward the injured captive. "You experiment on tiny kittens? Shall we do the same to you now?"

Locklear, his tears flowing freely, lifted the tiny Kzin kitten—a male—in hands that were tender, holding it to his breast. "It's breathing," he said. "A miracle, after getting the centrifuge treatment in a cage meant for something far bigger."

"Before I kill you, do something honorable," Scarface said to the wounded one. "Tell me where the other kitten is."

The captive pointed toward the end of the passage. "I am only an acolyte," he muttered. "I did not enjoy following orders."

Locklear sped along the cages and, at last, found Boot's female kitten revolving slowly in a cage of the proper size. He realized from the prominence of the tiny ribs that the kitten would cry for milk when it waked. *If* it waked. "Is she still alive?"

"Yes," the acolyte called back. "I am glad this happened. I can die with a less-troubled conscience."

After a hurried agreement and some rough questioning, they gave the acolyte a choice. He climbed into a cage hidden behind others at the end of another corridor and was soon revolving in stasis. The kittens went into one small cage. Working feverishly against the time when another enemy might walk into the crypt, they disassembled several more stasis cages and toted the working parts to the scooter, then added the kitten cage and, barely, levitated the scooter with its heavy load.

An hour later, Scarface bore the precious cage into the cave and Locklear, following with an armload of parts, heard the anguish of Boots. "They'll hear you from a hundred meters," he cautioned as Boots gathered the mewing, emaciated kittens in her arms.

They feared at first that her milk would no longer flow but presently, from where Boots had crept into the darkness, Kit returned. "They are suckling. Do not expect her to be much help from now on," Kit said.

Scarface checked the magazine of his sidearm. "One

priest has paid. There is no reason why I cannot extract full payment from the others now," he said.

"Yes, there is," Locklear replied, his fingers flying with hand tools from the cache. "Before you can get 'em all, they'll send devout fools to be killed while they escape. You said so yourself. Scarface, I don't want innocent Kzin blood on my hands! But after my old promise to Boots, I saw what that maniac was doing and—let's just say *my* honor was at stake." He knew that any modern Kzin commander would understand that. Setting down the wiring tool, he shuddered and waited until he could speak without a tremor in his voice. "If you'll help me get the wiring rigged for these stasis units, we can hide them in the right spot and take the entire bloody priesthood in one pile."

"All at once? I should like to know how," said Kit, counting the few units that lay around them.

"Well, I'll tell you how," said Locklear, his eyes bright with fervor. They heard him out, and then their faces glowed with the same zeal.

When their traps lay ready for emplacement, they slept while Kit kept watch. Long after dark, as Boots lay nearby cradling her kittens, Kit waked the others and served a cold broth. "You take a terrible chance, flying in the dark," she reminded them.

"We will move slowly," Scarface promised, "and the village fires shed enough light for me to land. Too bad about the senses of inferior species," he said, his ear umbrellas rising with his joke.

"How would you like a nice cold bath, tabby?" Locklear's question was mild, but it held an edge.

"Only monkeys *need* to bathe," said the Kzin, still amused. Together they carried their hardware outside and, by the light of a glowlamp, loaded the scooter while Kit watched for any telltale glow of eyes in the distance.

After a hurried nuzzle from Kit, Scarface brought the scooter up swiftly, switching the glowlamp to its pinpoint setting and using it as seldom as possible. Their forward motion was so slow that, on the two occasions when they blundered into the tops of towering fernpalms, they jettisoned nothing more than soft curses. An hour later, Scarface maneuvered them over a light yellow strip that became a heavily trodden path and began to follow that path by brief glowlamp flashes. The village, they knew, would eventually come into view.

It was Locklear who said, "Off to your right."

"The village fires? I saw them minutes ago."

"Oh shut up, supercat," Locklear grumped. "So where's our drop zone?"

"Near," was the reply, and Locklear felt their little craft swing to the side. At the pace of a weed seed, the scooter wafted down until Scarface, with one leg hanging through the viewslot of his craft, spat a short, nasty phrase. One quick flash of the lamp guided him to a level landing spot and then, with admirable panache, Scarface let the scooter settle without a creak.

If they were surprised now, only Scarface could pilot his scooter with any hope of getting them both away. Locklear grabbed one of the devices they had prepared and, feeling his way with only his feet, walked until he felt a rise of turf. Then he retraced his steps, vented a heavy sigh, and began the emplacement.

Ten minutes later he felt his way back to the scooter, tapping twice on one of its planks to avoid getting his head bitten off by an all-too-ready Scarface. "So far, so good," Locklear judged.

"This had better work," Scarface muttered.

"Tell me about it," said the retreating Locklear, grunting with a pair of stasis toroids. After the stasis units were all in place, Locklear rested at the scooter before creeping off again, this time with the glowlamp and a very sloppy wiring harness.

When he returned for the last time, he virtually fell onto the scooter. "It's all there," he said, exhausted, rubbing wrists still raw from his brief captivity. Scarface found his bearings again, but it was another hour before he floated up an arroyo and then used the lamp for a landing light.

He bore the sleeping Locklear into the cave as a man might carry a child. Soon they both were snoring, and Locklear did not hear the sound that terrified the distant villagers in late morning.

Locklear's first hint that his plans were in shreds
came with rough shaking by Scarface. "Wake up! The
monkeys have declared war," were the first words he
understood.

As they lay at the main cave entrance, they could see
sweeps of the pinnace as it moved over the Kzin village. Small energy beams lanced down several times, at
targets too widely spaced to be the huts. "They're tar-
geting whatever moves," Locklear ranted, pounding a
fist on hard turf. "And I'll bet the priests are hiding!"

Scarface brought up his all-band set and let it scan.
In moments, the voice of David Gomulka grated from the
speaker. ". . . kill 'em all. Tell 'em, Locklear! And when
they do let you go, you'd better be ready to talk; over."

"I can talk to 'em any time I like, you know," Locklear
said to his friend. "The set they gave me may have a
coded carrier wave."

"We must stop this terror raid," Scarface replied,
"before they kill us all!"

Locklear stripped his sidearm magazine of its rounds
and fingered the tiny ear set from its metal cage, screwing it into his ear. "Got me tied up," he said, trying to
ignore the disgusted look from Scarface at this un-
seemly lie. "Are you receiving . . ."

"We'll home in on your signal," Gomulka cut in.

Locklear quickly shoved the tiny set back into the
butt of his sidearm. "No, you won't," he muttered to
himself. Turning to Scarface: "We've got to transmit
from another place, or they'll triangulate on me."

Racing to the scooter, they fled to the arroyo and
skimmed the veldt to another spot. Then, still moving,
Locklear used the tiny set again. "Gomulka, they're
moving me."

The sergeant, furiously: "Where the fuck—?"

Locklear: "If you're shooting, let the naked savages
alone. The real tabbies are the ones with bandoliers,
got it? Bag 'em if you can but the naked ones aren't
combatants."

He put his little set away again but Scarface's unit, on
"receive only," picked up the reply. "Your goddamn

signal is shooting all over hell, Locklear. And whaddaya mean, not combatants? I've never had a chance to hunt tabbies like this. No little civilian shit is gonna tell us we can't teach 'em what it's like to be hunted! You got that, Locklear?"

They continued to monitor Gomulka, skating back near the cave until the scooter lay beneath spreading ferns. Fleeing into the safety of the cave, they agreed on a terrible necessity. "They intend to take ears and tails as trophies, or so they say," Locklear admitted. "You must find the most peaceable of your tribe, Boots, and bring them to the cave. They'll be cut down like so many vermin if you don't."

"No priests, and no acolytes," Scarface snarled. "Say nothing about us but you may warn them that no priest will leave this cave alive! That much, my honor requires."

"I understand," said Boots, whirling down one of the tunnels.

"And you and I," Scarface said to Locklear, "must lure that damned monkeyship away from this area. We cannot let them see Kzinti streaming in here."

In early afternoon, the scooter slid along rocky highlands before settling beneath a stone overhang. "The best cover for snipers on Kzersatz, Locklear. I kept my cache here, and I know every cranny and clearing. We just may trap that monkeyship, if I am clever enough at primitive skills."

"You want to trap them here? Nothing simpler," said Locklear, bringing out his tiny comm set.

But it was not to be so simple.

Locklear, lying in the open on his back with one hand under saffron vines, watched the pinnace thrum overhead. The clearing, ringed by tall fernpalms, was big enough for the *Anthony Wayne*, almost capacious for a pinnace. Locklear raised one hand in greeting as he counted four heads inside the canopy: Gomulka, Lee, Gazho, and Schmidt. Then he let his head fall back in pretended exhaustion, and waited.

In vain. The pinnace settled ten meters away, its engines still above idle, and the canopy levered up; but

the deserter crew had beam rifles trained on the sur-
rounding foliage and did not accept the bait. "They may
be back soon," Locklear shouted in Interworld. He
could hear the faint savage ripping at vegetation nearby,
and wondered if they heard it, too. "Hurry!"

"Tell us now, asshole," Gomulka boomed, his voice
coming both from the earpiece and the pinnace. "The
secret, *now*, or we leave you for the tabbies!"

Locklear licked his lips, buying seconds. "It's—It's
some kind of drive. The Outsiders built it here," he
groaned, wondering feverishly what the devil his tongue
was leading him into. He noted that Gazho and Lee
had turned toward him now, their eyes blazing with
greed. Schmidt, however, was studying the tallest
fernpalm, and suddenly fired a thin line of fire slashing
into its top, which was already shuddering.

"Not good enough, Locklear," Gomulka called. "We've
got great drives already. Tell us where it is."

"In a cavern. Other side of—valley," Locklear said,
taking his time. "Nobody has an—instantaneous drive
but Outsiders," he finished.

A whoop of delight, then, from Gomulka, one second
before that fernpalm began to topple. Schmidt was
already watching it, and screamed a warning in time for
the pilot to see the slender forest giant begin its agoniz-
ingly slow fall. Gomulka hit the panic button.

Too late. The pinnace, darting forward with its canopy
still up, rose to meet the spreading top of the tree
Scarface had cut using claws and fangs alone. As the
pinnace was borne to the ground, its canopy twisting
off its hinges, the swish of foliage and squeal of metal
filled the air. Locklear leaped aside, rolling away.

Among the yells of consternation, Gomulka's was loud-
est. "Schmidt, you dumb fuck!"

"It was him," Schmidt yelled, coming upright again
to train his rifle on Locklear—who fired first. If that
slug had hit squarely, Schmidt would have been dead
meat but its passage along Schmidt's forearm left only a
deep bloody crease.

Gomulka, every inch a warrior, let fly with his own
sidearm though his nose was bleeding from the impact.

But Locklear, now protected by another tree, returned
the fire and saw a hole appear in the canopy next to the
wide-staring eyes of Nathan Gazho.

When Scarface cut loose from thirty meters away,
Gomulka made the right decision. Yelling commands,
laying down a cover of fire first toward Locklear, then
toward Scarface, he drove his team out of the immobile
pinnace by sheer voice command while he peered past
the armored lip of the cockpit.

Scarface's call, in Kzin, probably could not be understood by the others, but Locklear could not have agreed
more. "Fight, run, fight again," came the snarling cry.

Five minutes later after racing downhill, Locklear
dropped behind one end of a fallen log and grinned at
Scarface, who lay at its other end. "Nice aim with that
tree."

"I despise chewing vegetable matter," was the reply.
"Do you think they can get that pinnace in operation
again?"

"With safety interlocks? It won't move at more than a
crawl until somebody repairs the—" but Locklear fell
silent at a sudden gesture.

From uphill, a stealthy movement as Gomulka scut-
tled behind a hillock. Then to their right, another brief
rush by Schmidt who held his rifle one-handed now.
This advance, basic to any team using projectile weapons, would soon overrun their quarry. The big blond
was in the act of dropping behind a fern when Scarface's
round caught him squarely in the breast, the rifle flying
away, and Locklear saw answering fire send tendrils of
smoke from his log. He was only a flicker behind Scarface,
firing blindly to force their heads down, as they bolted
downhill again in good cover.

Twice more, during the next hour, they opened up at
long range to slow Gomulka's team. At that range they
had no success. Later, drawing nearer to the village,
they lay behind stones at the lip of an arroyo. "With
only three," Scarface said with satisfaction. "They are
advancing more slowly."

"And we're wasting ammo," Locklear replied. "I have,
uh, two eights and four rounds left. You?"

"Eight and seven. Not enough against beam rifles."
The big Kzin twisted, then, ear umbrellas cocked toward
the village. He studied the sun's position, then came
to some internal decision and handed over ten of his
precious remaining rounds. "The brush in the arroyo's
throat looks flimsy, Locklear, but I could crawl under
its tops, so I know you can. Hold them up here, then
retreat under the brushtops in the arroyo and wait at its
mouth. With any luck I will reach you there."

The Kzin warrior was already leaping toward the
village. Locklear cried softly. "Where are you going?"

The reply was almost lost in the arroyo: "For reinforcements."

The sun had crept far across the sky of Kzersatz
before Locklear saw movement again, and when he did
it was nearly too late. A stone descended the arroyo,
whacking another stone with the crack of bowling balls;
Locklear realized that someone had already crossed the
arroyo. Then he saw Soichiro Lee ease his rifle into
sight. Lee simply had not spotted him.

Locklear took two-handed aim very slowly and fired
three rounds, full-auto. The first impact puffed dirt
into Lee's face so that Locklear did not see the others
clearly. It was enough that Lee's head blossomed, snapping up and back so hard it jerked his torso, and the
rifle clattered into the arroyo.

The call of alarm from Gazho was so near it spooked
Locklear into firing blindly. Then he was bounding into
the arroyo's throat, sliding into chest-high brush with
spreading tops.

Late shadows were his friends as he waited, hoping
one of the men would go for the beam rifle in plain
sight. Now and then he sat up and lobbed a stone into
brush not far from Lee's body. Twice, rifles scorched
that brush. Locklear knew better than to fire back
without a sure target while pinned in that ravine.

When they began sending heavy fire into the throat
of the arroyo, Locklear hoped they would exhaust their
plenums, but saw a shimmer of heat and knew his cover
could burn. He wriggled away downslope, past a trickle

of water, careful to avoid shaking the brush. It was then that he heard the heavy reports of a Kzin sidearm toward the village.

He nearly shot the rope-muscled Kzin that sprang into the ravine before recognizing Scarface, but within a minute they had worked their way together. "Those kshat priests," Scarface panted, "have harangued a dozen others into chasing me. I killed one priest; the others are staying safely behind."

"So where are our reinforcements?"

"The dark will transform them."

"But we'll be caught between enemies," Locklear pointed out.

"Who will engage each other in darkness, a dozen fools against three monkeys."

"Two," Locklear corrected. But he saw the logic now, and when the sunlight winked out a few minutes later he was watching the stealthy movement of Kzin acolytes along both lips of the arroyo.

Mouth close to Locklear's ear, Scarface said, "They will send someone up this watercourse. Move aside; my *wtsai* will deal with them quietly."

But when a military flare lit the upper reaches of the arroyo a few minutes later, they heard battle screams and suddenly, comically, two Kzin warriors came bounding directly between Locklear and Scarface. Erect, heads above the brushtops, they leapt toward the action and were gone in a moment.

Following with one hand on a furry arm, Locklear stumbled blindly to the arroyo lip and sat down to watch. Spears and torches hurtled from one side of the upper ravine while thin energy bursts lanced out from the other. Blazing brush lent a flickering light as well, and at least three great Kzin bodies surged across the arroyo toward their enemies.

"At times," Scarface said quietly as if to himself, "I think my species more valiant than stupid. But they do not even know their enemy, nor care."

"Same for those deserters," Locklear muttered, fascinated at the firefight his friend had provoked. "So how do we get back to the cave?"

"This way," Scarface said, tapping his nose, and set off with Locklear stumbling at his heels.

The cave seemed much smaller when crowded with a score of worried Kzinti, but not for long. The moment they realized that Kit was missing, Scarface demanded to know why.

"Two acolytes entered," explained one male, and Locklear recognized him as the mild-tempered Stalwart. "They argued three idiots into helping take her back to the village before dark."

Locklear, in quiet fury: "No one stopped them?"

Stalwart pointed to bloody welts on his arms and neck, then at a female lying curled on a grassy pallet. "I had no help but her. She tried to offer herself instead."

And then Scarface saw that it was Boots who was hurt but nursing her kittens in silence, and no cave could have held his rage. Screaming, snarling, claws raking tails, he sent the entire pack of refugees pelting into the night, to return home as best they could. It was Locklear's idea to let Stalwart remain; he had, after all, shed his blood in their cause.

Scarface did not subside until he saw Locklear, with the Kzin medkit, ministering to Boots. "A fine ally, but no expert in Kzin medicine," he scolded, choosing different unguents.

Boots, shamed at having permitted acolytes in the cave, pointed out that the traps had been disarmed for the flow of refugees. "The priesthood will surely be back here soon," she added.

"Not before afternoon," Stalwart said. "They never mount ceremonies during darkness. If I am any judge, they will drown the beauteous *prret* at high noon."

Locklear: "Don't they ever learn?"

Boots: "No. They are the priesthood," she said as if explaining everything, and Stalwart agreed.

"All the same," Scarface said, "they might do a better job this time. You," he said to Stalwart; "could you get to the village and back here in darkness?"

"If I cannot, call me acolyte. You would learn what they intend for your mate?"

"Of course he must," Locklear said, walking with him toward the main entrance. "But call before you enter again. We are setting deadly traps for anyone who tries to return, and you may as well spread the word."

Stalwart moved off into darkness, sniffing the breeze, and Locklear went from place to place, switching on traps while Scarface tended Boots. This tender care from a Kzin warrior might be explained as gratitude; even with her kittens, Boots had tried to substitute herself for Kit. Still, Locklear thought, there was more to it than that. He wondered about it until he fell asleep.

Twice during the night, they were roused by tremendous thumps and, once, a brief Kzin snarl. Scarface returned each time licking blood from his arms. The second time he said to a bleary-eyed Locklear, "We can plug the entrances with corpses if these acolytes keep squashing themselves against our ceilings." The grav polarizer traps, it seemed, made excellent sentries.

Locklear did not know when Stalwart returned but, when he awoke, the young Kzin was already speaking with Scarface. True to their rigid code, the priests fully intended to drown Kit again in a noon ceremony using heavier stones and, afterward, to lay siege to the cave.

"Let them; it will be empty," Scarface grunted. "Locklear, you have seen me pilot my little craft. I wonder . . ."

"Hardest part is getting around those deserters, if any," Locklear said. "I can cover a lot of ground when I'm fresh."

"Good. Can you navigate to where Boots had her birthing bower before noon?"

"If I can't, call me acolyte," Locklear said, smiling. He set off at a lope just after dawn, achingly alert. Anyone he met, now, would be a target.

After an hour, he was lost. He found his bearings from a promontory, loping longer, walking less, and was dizzy with fatigue when he climbed a low cliff to the overhang where Scarface had left his scooter. Breathing hard, he was lowering his rump to the scooter when the rifle butt whistled just over his head.

Nathan Gazho, who had located the scooter after scouring the area near the pinnace, felt fierce glee when he saw Locklear's approach. But he had not expected Locklear to drop so suddenly. He swung again as Locklear, almost as large as his opponent, darted in under the blow. Locklear grunted with the impact against his shoulder, caught the weapon by its barrel, and used it like a pry-bar with both hands though his left arm was growing numb. The rifle spun out of reach. As they struggled away from the ten-meter precipice, Gazho cursed—the first word by either man—and snatched his utility knife from its belt clasp, reeling back, his left forearm out. His crouch, the shifting of the knife, its extraordinary honed edge: marks of a man who had fought with knives before.

Locklear reached for the Kzin sidearm but he had placed it in a lefthand pocket and now that hand was numb. Gazho darted forward in a swordsman's balestra, flicking the knife in a short arc as he passed. By that time Locklear had snatched his own *wtsai* from its sheath with his right hand. Gazho saw the long blade but did not flinch, and Locklear knew he was running out of time. Standing four paces away, he pump-faked twice as if to throw the knife. Gazho's protecting forearm flashed to the vertical at the same instant when Locklear leaped forward, hurling the *wtsai* as he squatted to grasp a stone of fist size.

Because Locklear was no knife-thrower, the weapon did not hit point-first; but the heavy handle caught Gazho squarely on the temple and, as he stumbled back, Locklear's stone splintered his jaw. Nathan Gazho's legs buckled and inertia carried him backward over the precipice, screaming.

Locklear heard the heavy thump as he was fumbling for his sidearm. From above, he could see the broken body twitching, and his single round from the sidearm was more kindness than revenge. Trembling, massaging his left arm, he collected his *wtsai* and the beam rifle before crawling onto the scooter. Not until he levitated the little craft and guided it ineptly down the mountainside did he notice the familiar fittings of the standard-issue rifle. It had been fully discharged during the firefight, thanks to Scarface's tactic.

Many weeks before—it seemed a geologic age by now—Locklear had found Boots's private bower by accident. The little cave was hidden behind a low waterfall near the mouth of a shallow ravine, and once he had located that ravine from the air it was only a matter of following it, keeping low enough to avoid being seen from the Kzin village. The sun was almost directly overhead as Locklear approached the rendezvous. If he'd cut it too close . . .

Scarface waved him down near the falls and sprang onto the scooter before it could settle. "Let me fly it," he snarled, shoving Locklear aside in a way that suggested a Kzin on the edge of self-control. The scooter lunged forward and, as he hung on, Locklear told of Gazho's death.

"It will not matter," Scarface replied as he piloted the scooter higher, squinting toward the village, "if my mate dies this day." Then his predator's eyesight picked out the horrifying details, and he began to gnash his teeth in uncontrollable fury.

When they were within a kilometer of the village, Locklear could see what had pushed his friend beyond sanity. While most of the villagers stood back as if to distance themselves from this pomp and circumstance, the remaining acolytes bore a bound, struggling burden toward the lakeshore. Behind them marched the bandoliered priests, arms waving beribboned lances. They were chanting, a cacophony like metal chaff thrown into a power transformer, and Locklear shuddered.

Even at top speed, they would not arrive until that procession reached the walkway to deep water; and Kit, her limbs bound together with great stones for weights, would not be able to escape this time. "We'll have to go in after her," Locklear called into the wind.

"I cannot swim," cried Scarface, his eyes slitted.

"I can," said Locklear, taking great breaths to hoard oxygen. As he positioned himself for the leap, his friend began to fire his sidearm.

As the scooter swept lower and slower, one Kzin

priest crumpled. The rest saw the scooter and exhorted the acolytes forward. The hapless Kit was flung without further ceremony into deep water but, as he was leaping feet-first off the scooter, Locklear saw that she had spotted him. As he slammed into deep water, he could hear the full-automatic thunder of Scarface's weapon.

Misjudging his leap, Locklear let inertia carry him before striking out forward and down. His left arm was only at half-strength but the weight of his weapons helped carry him to the sandy bottom. Eyes open, he struggled to the one darker mass looming ahead.

But it was only a small boulder. Feeling the prickles of oxygen starvation across his back and scalp, he swiveled, kicking hard—and felt one foot strike something like fur. He wheeled, ignoring the demands of his lungs, wresting his *wtsai* out with one hand as he felt for cordage with the other. Three ferocious slices, and those cords were severed. He dropped the knife—the same weapon Kit herself had once dulled, then resharpened for him—and pushed off from the bottom in desperation.

He broke the surface, gasped twice, and saw a wide-eyed priest fling a lance in his direction. By sheer dumb luck, it missed, and after a last deep inhalation Locklear kicked toward the bottom again.

The last thing a wise man would do is locate a drowning tigress in deep water, but that is what Locklear did. Kit, no swimmer, literally climbed up his sodden flightsuit, forcing him into an underwater somersault, fine sand stinging his eyes. The next moment he was struggling toward the light again, disoriented and panicky.

He broke the surface, swam to a piling at the end of the walkway, and tried to hyperventilate for another hopeless foray after Kit. Then, between gasps, he heard a spitting cough echo in the space between the water's surface and the underside of the walkway. "Kit!" He swam forward, seeing her frightened gaze and her formidable claws locked into those rough planks, and patted her shoulder. Above them, someone was raising Kzin hell. "Stay here," he commanded, and kicked off toward the shallows.

He waded with his sidearm drawn. What he saw on

the walkway was abundant proof that the priesthood truly did not seem to learn very fast.

Five bodies sprawled where they had been shot, bleeding on the planks near deep water, but more of them lay curled on the planks within a few paces of the shore, piled atop one another. One last acolyte stood on the walkway, staring over the curled bodies. He was staring at Scarface, who stood on dry land with his own long *wtsai* held before him, snarling a challenge with eyes that held the light of madness. Then, despite what he had seen happen a half-dozen times in moments, the acolyte screamed and leaped.

Losing consciousness in midair, the acolyte fell heavily across his fellows and drew into a foetal crouch, as all the others had done when crossing the last six meters of planking toward shore. Those units Locklear had placed beneath the planks in darkness had kept three-ton herbivores in stasis, and worked even better on Kzinti. They'd known damned well the priesthood would be using the walkway again sooner or later; but they'd had no idea it would be *this* soon.

Scarface did not seem entirely sane again until he saw Kit wading from the water. Then he clasped his mate to him, ignoring the wetness he so despised. Asked how he managed to trip the gangswitch, Scarface replied, "You had told me it was on the inside of that piling, and those idiots did not try to stop me from wading to it."

"I noticed you were wet," said Locklear, smiling. "Sorry about that."

"I shall be wetter with blood presently," Scarface said with a grim look toward the pile of inert sleepers.

Locklear, aghast, opened his mouth.

But Kit placed her hand over it. "Rockear, I know you, and I know my mate. It is not your way but this is Kzersatz. Did you see what they did to the captive they took last night?"

"Big man, short black hair? His name is Gomulka."

"His name is meat. What they left of him hangs from a post yonder."

"Oh my god," Locklear mumbled, swallowing hard.

"But—look, just don't ask me to help execute anyone in stasis."

"Indeed." Scarface stood, stretched, and walked toward the piled bodies. "You may want to take a brief walk, Locklear," he said, picking up a discarded lance twice his length. "This is Kzin business, not monkey business." But he did not understand why, as Locklear strode away, the little man was laughing ruefully at the choice of words.

Locklear's arm was well enough, after two days, to let him dive for his *wtsai* while Kzinti villagers watched in curiosity—and perhaps in distaste. By that time they had buried their dead in a common plot and, with the help of Stalwart, begun to repair the pinnace's canopy holes and twisted hinges. The little hand-welder would have sped the job greatly but, Locklear promised, "We'll get it back. If we don't hit first, there'll be a stolen warship overhead with enough clout to fry us all."

Scarface had to agree. As the warrior who had overthrown the earlier regime, he now held not only the rights, but also the responsibilities of leading his people. Lounging on grassy beds in the village's meeting hut on the third night, they slurped hot stew and made plans. "Only the two of us can make that raid, you know," said the big Kzin.

"I was thinking of volunteers," said Locklear, who knew very well that Scarface would honor his wish if he made it a demand.

"If we had time to train them," Scarface replied. "But that ship could be searching for the pinnace at any moment. Only you and I can pilot the pinnace so, if we are lost in battle, those volunteers will be stranded forever among hostile monk—hostiles," he amended. "Nor can they use modern weapons."

"Stalwart probably could, he's a natural mechanic. I know Kit can use a weapon—not that I want her along."

"For a better reason than you know," Scarface agreed, his ears winking across the fire at the somnolent Kit.

"He is trying to say I will soon bear his kittens, Rockear," Kit said. "And please do not take Boots's new mate away merely because he can work magics with his hands." She saw the surprise in Locklear's face. "How could you miss that? He fought those acolytes in the cave for Boots's sake."

"I, uh, guess I've been pretty busy," Locklear admitted.

"We will be busier if that warship strikes before we do," Scarface reminded him. "I suggest we go as soon as it is light."

Locklear sat bolt upright. "Damn! If they hadn't taken my wristcomp—I keep forgetting. The schedules of those little suns aren't in synch; It's probably daylight there now, and we can find out by idling the pinnace near the force walls. You can damned well see whether it's light there."

"I would rather go in darkness," Scarface complained, "if we could master those night-vision sensors in the pinnace."

"Maybe, in time. I flew the thing here to the village, didn't I?"

"In daylight, after a fashion," Scarface said in a friendly insult, and flicked his sidearm from its holster to check its magazine. "Would you like to fly it again, right now?"

Kit saw the little man fill his hand as he checked his own weapon, and marveled at a creature with the courage to show such puny teeth in such a feral grin. "I know you must go," she said as they turned toward the door, and nuzzled the throat of her mate. "But what do we do if you fail?"

"You expect enemies with the biggest ship you ever saw," Locklear said. "And you know how those stasis traps work. Just remember, those people have night sensors and they can burn you from a distance."

Scarface patted her firm belly once. "Take great care," he said, and strode into darkness.

The pinnace's controls were simple, and Locklear's only worry was the thin chorus of whistles: air, escaping from a canopy that was not quite perfectly sealed. He briefed Scarface yet again as their craft carried them over Newduvai, and piloted the pinnace so that its re-entry thunder would roll gently, as far as possible from the *Anthony Wayne*.

It was late morning on Newduvai, and they could see

the gleam of the *Wayne*'s hull from afar. Locklear
slid the pinnace at a furtive pace, brushing spiny shrubs
for the last few kilometers before landing in a small
desert wadi. They pulled hinge pins from the canopy
and hid them in the pinnace to make its theft tedious.
Then, stuffing a roll of binder tape into his pocket,
Locklear began to trot toward his clearing.

"I am a kitten again," Scarface rejoiced, fairly floating
along in the reduced gravity of Newduvai. Then he
slowed, nose twitching. "Not far," he warned.

Locklear nodded, moved cautiously ahead, and then
sat behind a green thicket. Ahead lay the clearing with
the warship and cabin, seeming little changed—but a
heavy limb held the door shut as if to keep things in,
not out. And Scarface noticed two mansized craters just
outside the cabin's foundation logs. After ten minutes
without sound or movement from the clearing, Scarface
was ready to employ what he called the monkey ruse;
not quite a lie, but certainly a misdirection.

"Patience," Locklear counseled. "I thought you tabbies were hunters."

"Hunters, yes; not skulkers."

"No wonder you lose wars," Locklear muttered. But
after another half-hour in which they ghosted in deep
cover around the clearing, he too was ready to move.

The massive Kzin sighed, slid his *wtsai* to the rear
and handed over his sidearm, then dutifully held his
big pawlike hands out. Locklear wrapped the thin, bright
red binder tape around his friend's wrists many times,
then severed it with its special stylus. Scarface was
certain he could bite it through until he tried. Then he
was happy to let Locklear draw the stylus, with its
chemical enabler, across the tape where the slit could
not be seen. Then, hailing the clearing as he went, the
little man drew his own *wtsai* and prodded his "prisoner" toward the cabin.

His neck crawling with premonition, Locklear stood five
paces from the door and called again: "Hello, the cabin!"

From inside, several female voices and then only
one, which he knew very well: "Locklear go soon soon!"

"Ruth says that many times," he replied, half amused,

though he knew somehow that this time she feared for him. "New people keep gentles inside?"

Scarface, standing uneasily, had his ear umbrellas moving fore and aft. He mumbled something as, from inside, Ruth said, "Ruth teach new talk to gentles, get food. No teach, no food," she explained with vast economy.

"I'll see about that," he called and then, in Kzin, "what was that, Scarface?"

Low but urgent: "Behind us, fool."

Locklear turned. Not twenty paces away, Anse Parker was moving forward as silently as he could and now the hatchway of the *Anthony Wayne* yawned open. Parker's rifle hung from its sling but his service parabellum was leveled, and he was smirking. "If this don't beat all: my prisoner has a prisoner," he drawled.

For a frozen instant, Locklear feared the deserter had spied the *wtsai* hanging above Scarface's backside—but the Kzin's tail was erect, hiding the weapon. "Where are the others?" Locklear asked.

"Around. Pacifyin' the natives in that tabby lifeboat," Parker replied. "I'll ask you the same question, asshole."

The parabellum was not wavering. Locklear stepped away from his friend, who faced Parker so that the wrist tape was obvious. "Gomulka's boys are in trouble. Promised me amnesty if I'd come for help, and I brought a hostage," Locklear said.

Parker's movements were not fast, but so casual that Locklear was taken by surprise. The parabellum's short barrel whipped across his face, splitting his lip, bowling him over. Parker stood over him, sneering. "Buncha shit. If that happened, you'd hide out. You can tell a better one than that."

Locklear privately realized that Parker was right. And then Parker himself, who had turned half away from Scarface, made a discovery of his own. He discovered that, without moving one step, a Kzin could reach out a long way to stick the point of a *wtsai* against a man's throat. Parker froze.

"If you shoot me, you are deader than chivalry," Locklear said, propping himself up on an elbow. "Toss the pistol away."

Parker, cursing, did so, looking at Scarface, finding his chance as the Kzin glanced toward the weapon. Parker shied **away** with a sidelong leap, snatching for his slung rifle. And ignoring the leg of Locklear who tripped him nicely.

As his rifle tumbled into grass, Parker rolled to his feet and began sprinting for the warship two hundred meters away. Scarface outran him easily, then stationed himself in front of the warship's hatch. Locklear could not hear Parker's words, but his gestures toward the *wtsai* were clear: there ain't no justice.

Scarface understood. With that Kzin grin that so many humans failed to understand, he tossed the *wtsai* near Parker's feet in pure contempt. Parker grabbed the knife and saw his enemy's face, howled in fear, then raced into the forest, Scarface bounding lazily behind.

Locklear knocked the limb away from his cabin door and found Ruth inside with three others, all young females. He embraced the homely Ruth with great joy. The other young Neanderthalers disappeared from the clearing in seconds but Ruth walked off with Locklear. He had already seen the spider grenades that lay with sensors outspread just outside the cabin's walls. Two gentles had already died trying to dig their way out, she said.

He tried to prepare Ruth for his ally's appearance but, when Scarface reappeared with his *wtsai*, she needed time to adjust. "I don't see any blood," was Locklear's comment.

"The blood of cowards is distasteful," was the Kzin's wry response. "I believe you have my sidearm, friend Locklear."

They should have counted, said Locklear, on Stockton learning to fly the Kzin lifeboat. But lacking heavy weapons, it might not complicate their capture strategy too much. As it happened, the capture was more absurd than complicated.

Stockton brought the lifeboat bumbling down in late afternoon almost in the same depressions the craft's jackpads had made previously, within fifty paces of the *Anthony Wayne*. He and the lissome Grace wore holstered pistols, stretching out their muscle kinks as they walked toward the bigger craft, unaware that they were being watched. "Anse; we're back," Stockton shouted. "Any word from Gomulka?"

Silence from the ship, though its hatch steps were down. Grace shrugged, then glanced at Locklear's cabin. "The door prop is down, Curt. He's trying to hump those animals again."

"Damn him," Stockton railed, and both turned toward the cabin. To Grace he complained, "If you were a better lay, he wouldn't always be—*good God!*"

The source of his alarm was a long blood-chilling, gut-wrenching scream. A Kzin scream, the kind featured in horror holovision productions; and very, very near. "Battle stations, red alert, up ship," Stockton cried, bolting for the hatch.

Briefly, he had his pistol ready but had to grip it in his teeth as he reached for the hatch rails of the *Anthony Wayne*. For that one moment he almost resembled a piratical man of action, and that was the moment when he stopped, one foot on the top step, and Grace bumped her head against his rump as she fled up those steps.

"I don't think so," said Locklear softly. To Curt Stockton, the muzzle of that alien sidearm so near must have looked like a torpedo launcher. His face drained of color, the commander allowed Locklear to take the pistol from his trembling lips. "And Grace," Locklear went on, because he could not see her past Stockton's bulk, "I doubt if it's your style anyway, but don't give your pistol a second thought. That Kzin you heard? Well, they're out there behind you, but they aren't in here. Toss your parabellum away and I'll let you in."

Late the next afternoon they finished walling up the crypt on Newduvai, with a small work force of willing hands recruited by Ruth. As the little group of gentles filed away down the hillside, Scarface nodded toward the rubble-choked entrance. "I still believe we should have executed those two, Locklear."

"I know you do. But they'll keep in stasis for as long as the war lasts, and on Newduvai— Well, Ruth's people agree with me that there's been enough killing."

Locklear turned his back on the crypt and Ruth moved to his side, still wary of the huge alien whose speech sounded like the sizzle of fat on a skewer.

"Your ways are strange," said the Kzin, as they walked toward the nearby pinnace. "I know something of Interworld beauty standards. As long as you want that female lieutenant alive, it seems to me you would keep her, um, available."

"Grace Agostinho's beauty is all on the outside. And there's a girl hiding somewhere on Newduvai that those deserters never did catch. In a few years she'll be— Well, you'll meet her someday." Locklear put an arm around Ruth's waist and grinned. "The truth is, Ruth thinks *I'm* pretty funny-looking, but some things you can learn to overlook."

At the clearing, Ruth hopped from the pinnace first. "Ruth will fix place nice, like before," she promised, and walked to the cabin.

"She's learning Interworld fast," Locklear said proudly. "Her telepathy helps—in a lot of ways. Scarface, do you realize that her people may be the most tremendous discovery of modern times? And the irony of it! The empathy these people share probably helped isolate them from the modern humans that came from their own gene pool. Yet their kind of empathy might be the only viable future for us." He sighed and stepped to the turf. "Sometimes I wonder whether I want to be found."

Standing beside the pinnace, they gazed at the *Anthony Wayne*. Scarface said, "With that warship, you could do the finding."

Locklear assessed the longing in the face of the big Kzin. "I know how you feel about piloting, Scarface. But you must accept that I can't let you have any craft more advanced than your scooter back on Kzersatz."

"But— Surely, the pinnace or my own lifeboat?"

"You see that?" Locklear pointed toward the forest.

Scarface looked dutifully away, then back, and when he saw the sidearm pointing at his breast, a look of terrible loss crossed his face. "I see that I will never understand you," he growled, clasping his hands behind his head. "And I see that you still doubt my honor."

Locklear forced him to lean against the pinnace, arms behind his back, and secured his hands with binder tape. "Sorry, but I have to do this," he said. "Now get back in the pinnace. I'm taking you to Kzersata."

"But I would have—"

"Don't say it," Locklear demanded. "Don't tell me what you want, and don't remind me of your honor, goddammit! Look here, I *know* you don't lie. And what if the next ship here is another Kzin ship? You won't lie to them either, your bloody honor won't let you. They'll find you sitting pretty on Kzersatz, right?"

Teetering off-balance as he climbed into the pinnace without using his arms, Scarface still glowered. But after a moment he admitted, "Correct."

"They won't court-martial you, Scarface. Because a lying, sneaking monkey pulled a gun on you, tied you up, and sent you back to prison. I'm telling you here and now, I see Kzersatz as a prison and every tabby on this planet will be locked up there for the duration of the war!" With that, Locklear sealed the canopy and made a quick check of the console read-outs. He reached across to adjust the inertia-reel harness of his companion, then shrugged into his own. "You have no choice, and no tabby telepath can ever claim you did. *Now* do you understand?"

The big Kzin was looking below as the forest dropped away, but Locklear could see his ears forming the Kzin equivalent of a smile. "No wonder you win wars," said Scarface.

Introduction

Herein Lois Bjold, *whose* Falling Free *is this year's winner of the Nebula Award for Best Science Fiction or Fantasy Novel, gives us an example of the kind of thinking about science fiction that leads to science fiction awards. To quote Roland Green's review of her novel* Brothers in Arms *in the* Chicago Sun-Times: *"Read, or you will be missing something extraordinary."*

ALLEGORIES OF CHANGE:

The "New" Biotech in the Eye of Science Fiction

Lois McMaster Bujold

Cloning. Organ transplants. Surrogate mothers. *In vitro* gestation, babies from "replicators". Bioengineering of animals. Life from the lab. New ideas, the earnest newspaper reporter asks?

No—old ones. Very old ones, in some cases. For

example, *in vitro* gestation—and cloning—was used by Aldous Huxley in his novel *Brave New World*, published in 1932, almost 60 years ago. Bioengineering of animals? *The Island of Doctor Moreau* by H. G. Wells was published in 1896. Human organ transplant was explored by writer Cordwainer Smith in one of a remarkable series of short stories in the 1950s. In Smith's "A Planet Named Shayol," prisoners are used as living organ banks, given a virus that causes duplicate organs to grow which are then "harvested" for the medical centers to transplant. Life from the lab is one of the oldest ideas of all—Mary Shelley's classic *Frankenstein* was published in 1818, over 170 years ago.

Even the least alert person must begin to notice that the problems that are now suddenly puzzling ethicists, lawyers, and legislators—and, in a democracy, the public—have been discussed in an on-going forum for more than a hundred years. That dialogue is called science fiction. And biology has been one of the sciences in science fiction from the very beginning.

It is important first to note that science fiction and science are not the same thing. Science has its own momentum, and will proceed largely independently of speculation about it. Yet science is not separate from us; it's something *people* do. Science fiction is literature; it's storytelling. And the stories we tell are about ourselves.

All fiction is psychological allegory, myth, a morality play on some level. But science fiction deals especially with allegories of change. And change is the hallmark of our age.

Science fiction has always been secretly about our own stresses, in the present, whichever present that was. For most of the 20th century, this has been a present visibly and stressfully in process of becoming the future. So some SF can become outdated and archaic; science fictional allegories based on the social concerns of the 1950s can fall strangely on the ear today. But these love letters weren't addressed to the future, but to their own times. It continues so today.

My favorite type of SF story thrusts the hero not just

into technical difficulties or a simple conflict between good and evil, but into genuine moral dilemmas jumping out at him from some unanticipated change. To me, these grey areas are the most arresting. You don't even need a villain to make your story go (though villains are also a part of what makes a story a relief from real life, someone outside ourselves we can *blame* our troubles on, oh boy!). There is more fascination in a conflict between two competing, mutually exclusive goods.

Now, the new biotechnology is an absolute gold mine of such ethical dilemmas, and therefore would appear a source of resonant story ideas.

However, the non-SF-reader may be surprised to learn that I do not cull my story ideas directly from the news, not even the science news. Remember how old that news is? True, some science background is a part of my daily life. But for my novel *Ethan of Athos*, set on a planet where babies are routinely gestated in vats, my research consisted only of talking with an M.D. about the pineal gland, looking up some pharmacological facts about a certain amino acid, and re-reading the article on embryology from my old college anatomy textbook—did the placenta arise from maternal or fetal tissue? It made a difference in the design of my "uterine replicators," the aforementioned baby vats.

But the important thing about the uterine replicators was not how they worked (Huxley had the essentials figured out 60 years ago, and embryology hasn't changed since then), but how their fact of their existence might fundamentally change the ways people could live, ways that even Huxley had overlooked.

The first thing that sprang to my mind (as a veteran of several Lamaze classes) was that the existence of this technology could break the female monopoly on reproduction. For the first time in history, it might be possible to have an all-male society that wasn't sterile. All-male societies exist in our world—armies, prisons, and monasteries to name just three, but they must constantly be renewed from outside. Since armies and especially prisons tend to have skewed, abnormally violent populations, I chose the monastery model as the most stable basis for my projected society, as my title reveals (the real monastery peninsula of Athos in Greece, after which I named my fictional planet, has been forbidden to women for over a thousand years).

But co-equal with technology and history in the springs of that book was science fiction itself. I had simply read one too many really bad Amazon Planet stories from the 1950s, in which (usually male) writers concentrated on images of women in an all-female society fumbling around in male roles such as soldiering. (I leave as an exercise for the student the consideration of the 1950s as a society shuddering on the verge of women's lib.) Okay, I growled, let's turn this thing on its head. How well would men do taking over women's roles? There promptly arose my quintessential Athosian hero, Dr. Ethan Urquhart, an obstetrician, whose job it was to be (technologically) pregnant for his planet by running a Reproduction Center. (A Reproduction Center, as its name should imply, is a fetus farm, an Athosian medical facility where the good citizen goes to drop off his sperm sample at the Paternity Ward, and returns nine months later to pick up his son. Or maybe they deliver.)

I might mention the novel also includes a bioengineered telepath on the run from his rather nasty military-research creators, a female space mercenary, stolen genes, the ultimate truth drug, the effect the closed ecology of a huge space station has on its funeral practices, and of course don't forget the mutant newts. Which hints at the real, true reason for the existence of science fiction; we're doing this for *fun*. I had a blast writing that book.

Science fiction does this sort of thing all the time. A lively source of story ideas is a game called, "Let's Extrapolate This Trend To Absurdity." I played a short round of it with Canadian SF writer S. M. Stirling, over lunch at a convention last year.

We began with the question, what unexpected thing that nobody's written yet would really happen if medicine cracked human immortality, or at least vastly extended human lifespan (a hoary theme). I noted at once that most new ideas in science take over not because their hot young originators change their teachers' minds (a human mind is monumentally harder to change than a bed), but because they *outlive* the old geezers and take over their tenure. Therefore extended lifespan would result in a slowing of the pace of scientific progress. Further, by a natural process of accumulation the old folks would eventually end up owning everything, turning the generation gap into an economic class division. The only way a young person could get ahead would be to get away.

Into this pot we threw faster-than-light travel and the colonization of space, and stirred vigorously. There immediately resulted a structure of human society in which young people and scientific advance move outward from Earth in a concentric sphere of colonies, each hardening in its turn. The leading edge really would *be* out on the edge, with the whole social history of the human race fossilized in layers behind it. Presto, a whole new science fiction universe to play with and set stories in.

A different and more dystopian universe results by changing that initial parameter of "escapability"—suppose this society is stuck on Earth? Then the only way for a young person to get ahead becomes to violently remove the older person occupying the next space. The generation gap becomes the generation war, the ultimate defense from the next generation being mandatory sterility. And suppose somebody wanted to change that system. And suppose . . . And what if . . . .

And it was no accident that this whole chain of reasoning occurred to a couple of middle-aged babyboomers, moving with the rest of their pig through the python and watching the aging of America. Psychological allegory for our times.

The secret of the "sudden" development of biological themes in SF is of course that they aren't sudden at all. They've been there all the time but, like latent extremes in any varied population, are being called forth to prominence by pressures of the environment. SF hasn't just now discovered the existence of biotechnology, but the world at large has, and so is making stories on the subject newly popular.

Unfortunately, the moral dilemmas of the new biotech are not to be resolved in fiction. Actual morality is solely a function of individuals possessed of free will operating in the one and only present reality. Fiction can talk, play, illuminate, teach, spot traps, suggest alternatives. It is not the arena of action.

As a writer, I regard the whole chaotic prospect of the new biotech with a certain gleeful relish. But as a citizen I am not quite so gung-ho. My sympathy is great for the people who must really live through these present dilemmas. Nevertheless, I am a cautious optimist about the new biotechnologies, and technology in general. Thanks to the very pace of change which plagues us, not all problems have to be solved. Some can be out-lived.

Consider the thorny agony of organ transplants. At present it is a simple fact that one person must die for the next to live. But the terrible ethical problems of allocation will not have to be resolved, if they can be leap-frogged instead by new technologies of artifical mechanical or (shades of Cordwainer Smith) laboratory-grown organs. Then there would be plenty for everyone. This is an example of a transitional dilemma, tough on those caught in the gears during the change-over, but not requiring long-term social solutions.

But other kinds of problems are not self-solving, and it is vital to discern which is which. Consider the creation of biological weapons whose only purpose is the destruction of human beings, and the horrifying possibilities of their accidental or deliberate release. The abuse of technology for vile purposes is not a problem that can be resolved by the application of more and better technology. Technology can make us healthy and wealthy, it cannot make us wise.

Of course, we won't grow wise if we fail to think about or notice what we're doing. And not all thought has to be dull.

A "thought experiment" is science's approach to phenomena that are too large, complex, uncontrollable or inaccessable for laboratory experiment: events in the interior of the sun, say, or in human society. The trick is to rigorously follow out the logic of one's theory and then cross-check and see if the results match observed reality. Science fiction too can be a kind of thought experiment, about human behavior and culture.

Science fiction is the playground of the intellect, but the play can get very serious. The minute we go beyond the simplest gadget story, we're into just such thought experiments. Badly designed thought experiments will yield false results just like badly designed laboratory experiments. (I'm reminded of the joke about experiment design: in a single-blind study, the patient doesn't know if he's getting the drug or the placebo. In the double-blind study, the doctor doesn't know either. And in the triple-blind experiment, the administrator has lost the key that told which was which.) The reader would gain, I fear, some rather peculiar insights into the human condition from a steady reading diet of, say, the SF sub-genre of men's-adventure post-holocaust blood porn. The images generated are arresting (hence very saleable), but it's crocodile-brain allegory. Garbage in, garbage out.

But at the other end of the spectrum are works such as the award-winning *A Door Into Ocean* (Arbor House, 1986) by Dr. Joan Slonczewski, one of Ohio's two Quaker science fiction writers and a working genetic engineer. Her book has it all—world-building, breathtaking scientific speculation (she does marvellous and subtle things with the potential of information storage and retrieval from biological systems) and an underlying humane vision of great beauty. The society of alien Sharers, based on an enormously sophisticated biotechnology, that she projects is both mirror and extension of her own most deeply held convictions and highest hopes for human goodness. The Sharers are tested near to destruction, yet never yield to the temptations of violence, stupidity, or fear. Now there's an allegory worth taking in, a pattern for behavior quite worthy of new myth.

Myth, driven out of mainstream literature by the ascendance of "realism" for most of the 20th century, has found firm refuge in SF. The function of myth, of psychological allegory, is to feed a hunger not for facts but for meaning. We want to *understand* the torrent of change in which we are swimming (or drowning.) What is it and what does it mean and where do we go from here, and what raft of reason can we cling to and how do we stay human in the best sense? So I don't worry about science "catching up" with science fiction and leaving it bereft of topics, because I don't see SF as "about" science, but rather as about human response to science-driven change. And that is a dance of infinite variety and suprise.

ELIZABETH MOON

Anne McCaffrey on Elizabeth Moon:

"She's a damn fine writer. The Deed of Pak-senarrion is fascinating. I'd use her book for research if I ever need a woman warrior. I know how they train now. We need more like this."

By the Compton Crook Award winning author of the Best First Novel of the Year

Sheepfarmer's Daughter
65416-0 • 512 pages • $3.95 _____

Divided Allegiance
69786-2 • 528 pages • $3.95 _____

Oath of Gold
69798-6 • 512 pages • $3.95 _____

Introduction

After The Fall we will all immediately come to our senses, put our collective shoulders to the wheel, and work together to create a New World, one that will combine the knowledge and power of the Old with the spirit of cooperation and fellow-feeling born in the New. Right?

Nah! No matter how bad things are the ones on top will figure that any change is for the worse, since they probably won't be on top any more. Just ask the Prez.

REST IN PEACE

Kevin J. Anderson

I

Every shadowy corner hides a thousand assassins.

Prez Siroth stopped suddenly in the darkness just inside the crumbling catacombs. He narrowed his eyes. He sniffed the air, drawing in the earthy scent of shadows, the lingering smells that would attract rats.

The guards quickly stumbled to a halt to avoid running into Siroth, then backtracked to form a protective ring around him. In the dim torchlight, Siroth could see that their eyes had gone wide. "What is it, my Prez?" asked the captain of the guard.

With ice-blue eyes, Siroth gazed silently into the broken tunnels for a moment longer. Wispy long hair hung to his shoulders, untrimmed. Sacks of grain had been piled up against the collapsing walls to shore them up against negligence. In the older sections of the tunnels, worn and fragmented flagstones lined the floors . . . but the newly dug catacombs offered only hard-packed dirt, which might easily muffle the footsteps of someone in hiding.

"Light two more torches." Siroth turned to glare at

the fat, dirty man leading them deeper into the tunnels. "And if *he* makes a single unexpected move—slit his throat." Siroth's lips curved in a snarl/smile.

Rathsell, the fat man, tittered nervously. "You are too suspicious, my Prez."

"I have held my reign for *six years* now. You can never be too suspicious!"

"Nothing to fear from me, my Prez. Wait until you see what the children dug up. It's a great discovery!" Behind fat Rathsell's grin, Siroth could see the splotchy red of anxiety on the man's face.

"Children? I left *you* in charge of storing grain down here—"

"Oh yes, my Prez! But the children stay in here to kill the rats and to dig out more tunnels. You can be sure I gave them a sound beating when I learned they never told me about the vault they found. And then I came to you without delay!"

Siroth's voice was cold. "Why would you come to tell *me*?"

Caught off guard, Rathsell smeared his palms on his worn and dirty trousers. He wore no shirt to cover his folds of fat; a clean red barrette was clipped to his ear as an ornament. "I . . . um, well, my Prez, there are some who would pay great rewards for something like this. . . ."

Siroth scowled. "What's so special about this vault?"

Fat Rathsell's eyes lit up, as if he was about to share the secrets of the universe. "It is from *Before*!"

"So are all the old buildings." The Prez sounded bored.

"But this vault is untouched!"

"If it isn't worth my while, I'm going to let Grull play with you."

A flicker of terror passed across the fat man's eyes, but he forced another smile. "It *will* be worth your while, my Prez."

Their footsteps suddenly became muffled as they passed from the last flagstones to the bare earth of the new tunnels. The shadows grew deeper.

"What can you possibly want with a reward? You already have more than you deserve here."

Siroth saw that fat Rathsell was struggling to put on his kindest face. "You may remember, my Prez, how ugly a woman my wife is, with three arms and all. With a nice reward, perhaps I can buy myself a prettier one. That's all I want with my humble life."

"Uh-huh," Siroth said.

Suddenly the Prez's heart twisted into knots, clenching and thumping as if choking on an air pocket. Pain shot through his chest, radiating like electrified wires from his sternum. He held his breath. He kept his face molded in a mask of self-control, showing nothing. Bloodwind roared in his ears; flecks of color tinged with black swirled behind his eyes. His mind began to pound, and he felt like he was rising, floating, swallowed up in a great maw more deadly than any assassin's knife. Siroth gritted his teeth as Rathsell led him onward, with the guards close behind. The Prez fought with himself not to stumble. He reached inside his tunic and massaged the long, lumpy scar in the center of his chest until the pain subsided.

Again? Already? he thought to himself, *I should have known a peasant's heart wouldn't last more than two years.*

The pain backed off again, momentarily tamed, and Siroth strode forward with a grim enthusiasm he hadn't felt in a long time. The undulating torchlight reflected off a metal door set into the left wall as they turned a corner. Rathsell made a show of opening the heavy door. The guards stood tense and silent. He gestured for Siroth to enter. "My Prez—?"

"No. You go first. Then three guards. Then I'll come. The rest of the guards will follow me."

Rathsell hastily agreed and entered the vault as pale light began to flow automatically from darkened plates along the interior walls. The guards uttered their astonishment as they followed. Siroth came next, trying to adjust his eyes to the light splashing on his face.

The Prez forcibly resisted expressing his awe. The glistening walls of the chamber were a polished white, cleaner than anything he had seen in his entire life. The faint, not-unpleasant smell of ammonia and chemicals floated just at the limits of perception, driving back the odors of dirt and mustiness from the catacombs. The floor of the chamber, though hard, somehow swallowed the sound of his footsteps as he walked farther into the room.

Most of the crowded floor space was taken up by eight oblong cases like crystalline coffins. Each contained a motionless human form. Siroth stepped cautiously among them, looking through the transparent walls. The bodies inside seemed like wax sculptures, pale, not breathing . . . dead? for an undefinable reason, Siroth didn't think so.

The guards stood in silent awe, and Rathsell rubbed his hands together in delight. The fat man ran mumbling among the machines along one wall, closely inspecting a series of lights lazily pulsing on and off, as if he knew what he was doing. Siroth didn't like the look of Rathsell's confidence. Beside each of the coffins squatted a bulky control box that appeared to monitor the unmoving figure within.

One crystal coffin had been positioned slightly in front of the other seven, and Siroth moved slowly toward it, running his fingertips along the polished surfaces of the glass cases. The central human looked like a god come to Earth: his perfect face was capped with delicately styled black curls, and his physique was large and muscular, seeming to radiate power, even helpless as he was. The Prez rapped his knuckles on the glass in defiance, to show his own superiority.

"Do you like that one, my Prez?" Rathsell said. The fat man's eyes gleamed and his chins bobbed in a disgusting way. "I can make him speak to you. Watch—he can talk even while he's asleep!"

Intoxicated with his own good fortune, Rathsell rushed to a console under a blank patch on the wall opposite Siroth. Making certain the Prez was looking, Rathsell singled out a large green button surrounded by inward-pointing arrows; it simply cried out to be pushed, and Rathsell obliged.

Images began to form within the depths of the screen, rapidly crystallizing into a picture of the eight sleepers—

awake now—standing together in spring-green jumpsuits and each bearing gleaming eyes and a blank smile. The picture made Siroth think of the old family photographs that scavengers sometimes burned in their hovels because the fumes made them feel lightheaded.

The godlike man with the dark hair stepped forward, looking out of the screen with gleaming black eyes as deep as the universe. The Prez stifled a shiver.

"Greetings, men of the future. If you have come to witness our awakening, we welcome you in peace and friendship. You will not remember us, for we are merely dreamers and have left no record of ourselves behind."

The leader smiled, pausing for a breath. The others smiled as well. "I am Draigen, and these seven others are with me: a surgeon, an artist, an agricultural engineer, an historian, a singer, a mathematician, a writer. We come from a troubled time, with many needs and many problems. But we could see that this bureaucratic nemesis was dying at its core, strangled in its own red tape, lost within its own intricacies. Within a century, the serpent would have finished devouring itself. We had to *wait* until nothing would hinder us from doing what we had been called to do."

Siroth found the man's voice charismatic, dangerous. Draigen's words seemed laced with fever, and his dark eyes glistened. The other green-suited dreamers stood behind him as if in awe of their leader's vision.

"We collected our knowledge and all the tools we would need to reshape our world after the demise of bureaucracy—and came here to slumber for a hundred years. Now we shall help *you* to rebuild the world as it was meant to be, without oppression, without cruelty, with freedom and justice for all mankind!"

The tape finished, and the shining white wall absorbed the image. Siroth stood motionless, pondering, with a distasteful smirk locked on his face.

He silently reached out to take a stainless-steel club from the nearest guard and hefted the heavy pipe in his hand. He stepped over to Draigen's case, looking down at the strangely impotent form of the dreamer. Siroth swung the pipe down, smashing the crystal coffin above the dark-haired dreamer's face.

The Prez smiled.

Siroth took a calculated breath before he went berserk, plunging from one case to the next, smashing them, swinging the club down to crush the monitor-computers, hurling the pipe like a spear through the screen at the far wall. He kicked at shards of crystal, dodging sparks and plunging through smoke.

The guards watched dispassionately. Fat Rathsell sobbed in horror, confusion, and genuine loss. He might have wanted to stop the Prez, but he dared not.

Panting, Siroth picked up the club again and casually handed it back to the guard. The rebellious pain behind his sternum returned, but he had more important things to attend to. He tried to ignore the pain, mentally and uselessly cursing his heart. But the pounding knives in his chest remained.

Siroth turned his cold eyes on Rathsell, motioning to the guards. "Take him away and execute him. For most vile treason!"

Rathsell's face blanched to a pasty white, as if his skin had just turned into gruel. The guards grabbed his arms and began to drag him out. The fat man struggled in disbelief and confusion, but his feet found no purchase on the polished white floor. The decorative red barrette dropped from his ear.

Siroth held up a hand. "But kill him *quickly*. That's his reward."

Rathsell made other sounds, but could form no coherent words.

In the shadows of the catacombs, haggard and dirt-encrusted children with eyes sunken from near starvation watched Rathsell's plight, and snickered.

Forgetting all else, Siroth stared down into the crystalline case containing Draigen's body. Tiny flecks of broken glass frosted the dreamer's brow like snowflakes, but otherwise the body was unharmed. The Prez reached out to touch Draigen's large, muscular arm, admiring the lean body. The mold for this one had been shattered long ago in the holocaust.

Rathsell's screams reverberated through the winding catacombs, then abruptly stopped.

The convulsive pain in Siroth's chest took a long time to subside, but he managed to smile as he ran his fingernail on Draigen's motionless breastbone. "Such a helpful dreamer. I may be able to use you after all."

II

Deep in the Prez's chambers, the blind old man sat in front of a crackling fire, letting the warmth bathe his face. He heard one branch, somewhere near the back, settle heavily into the ash. The wood snapped and sputtered as it burned. It smelled a little green.

He felt a disturbance in the room, the barely noticed shifting of air currents. He tensed, trying to restrain his smile. "You sound weary, Siroth."

He heard the Prez slap his hand down on the table-top in exasperation and defeat. "Dammit, Grull! How did you know it was me?"

"Your breathing is very distinctive. Look on the tabletop at the new device I designed."

The Prez looked at the scattered papers on the table. Grull stood up from the chair by the fire and unerringly found his way over to Siroth.

"See, the loops fit around the victim's fingers, toes, wrists and ankles, and are then attached to those wheels of varying sizes in such a way that merely by turning the wheels we can wrench every finger, every toe out of joint, one by one, until we have achieved the desired results."

Siroth nodded. "You still have trouble closing up your circles, Grull." He dropped the sketch back on the tabletop and went to sit in the old man's chair by the fire. The Prez cracked his knuckles as he watched the firelight. "What happened while I was gone?"

"Well, the fukkups staged another revolt, trying to break out of their pen and clamoring to be freed, again. They said they wanted to see you."

"And?"

"Three of them seemed to be the instigators. I had

them strung upside down over the pens and then burned alive. The rest calmed down."

"Anything else?"

"Well, two men rode up, emissaries from Prez Claysus."

"That water-spined fairy!" Siroth snorted.

"Remember Praetoth, the architect who rebuilt your castle when it collapsed two years ago? You've still got him in the dungeons, you know. It seems the home of Prez Claysus has likewise fallen in on itself, and his emissaries are 'honorably requesting' that we should work together for the common good of all. Claysus wants to borrow our architect."

Siroth laughed. "That sounds exactly like him! have you replied yet?"

Grull smiled broadly. "I tied the emissaries backwards onto their horses with their own entrails, and sent them back."

"A straightforward enough answer."

Grull made his way back to the chair beside the fire, found that Siroth was already sitting in it, and scowled as he paced the room instead. "So what did Rathsell want?"

The Prez briefly explained about the vault from *Before*, the dreamers, and how he had destroyed the apparatus.

"A wise decision, my Prez. We don't want any empire-building dreamers from *Before* ruining all you've done. Everything in that vault should be burned."

"No." Grull detected a pensive note in Siroth's voice, though he could not see the expression on the other's face. "I have saved them, especially their leader. I want his heart. And you can have his eyes."

Grull bit his breath back, stunned. Siroth rarely surprised him anymore.

"Doctor Sero has given me one new heart, but it is already dying. And now, with this godlike dreamer's heart . . . I will be *strong*! You should see him, Grull! He's perfect. Up until now you said you wouldn't have new eyes if they had to come from a peasant, or from a fukkup who had five or six extra eyes. But now it's *perfect*! You'll have your sight back, Grull. After sixty years."

The blind old man sat in silence, thinking about sight and Siroth's not-quite-correct reasons as to why he had denied new eyes before. Grull had lost his sight during the holocaust, six decades before. He had never looked upon what *After* was like. He wasn't sure he wanted to.

III

The dark-haired dreamer lay on the surgical table, stretched out like a mannequin as Doctor Sero inspected him disdainfully. Rigor had shut Draigen's black eyes, trapping his Utopian visions beneath the thin lids. Later, before the body could begin to spoil, the doctor would have to cut those eyes out and preserve them for Grull.

Siroth turned his head and sat up on another surgical table beside Draigen's. "Are you about ready, Sero?"

The doctor looked up from his assortment of medical tools, staring with swollen, buglike eyes. "Yes, my Prez."

"And you *will* be successful?"

"I was successful the last time. You're a quick-healer, Prez Siroth. I explained it all to you before—the chromosome-scrambling viruses that filled the air after the holocaust poisoned our gene pool. Most of the aberrations turned out like the fukkups, but what went wrong with them, went *right* with you. You know what happens whenever you get injured." The doctor's voice betrayed his own lack of interest in the lecture, in the upcoming operation, and in the Prez himself.

"I've been practicing this operation for the past week. Out of ten tries, three have survived. All three were quick-healers."

Sero ran a finger along the scar on Siroth's bare chest, thinking how much it reminded him of an artist's signature on a masterpiece. His father had been a great surgeon from *Before* who had taught Sero from the books and implements found in the old buildings. But his father hadn't been good enough to heal himself of his own death wound. And now Sero had to discover all the lost surgical arts by hit-or-miss vivisection.

The Prez narrowed his eyes and reached out to snatch

the doctor's fingers away from the old scar, holding them in a brutal grip with his clenched fist. "Grull will be here with my guards during the operation," he hissed.

"My father used to say a surgeon's hands are sacred things, never to be touched by another," Sero said almost offhandedly. "My dear Prez, if I saw you were about to die during this operation, I'd plunge a scalpel deep into my own throat, rather than let Grull touch me."

Siroth stiffened, and the doctor pushed him flat on the table. "But *relax*, my Prez. When you awaken, you'll have the heart of the biggest dreamer of all!"

"What a horrible thought . . ." Siroth muttered.

His eyes took so long to focus.

An apparition stood in front of him, dressed in the spring-green uniform of the dreamers. Draigen! No . . . one of the others in the tape, one who had lain sleeping at the far end of the vault. The dreamer's eyes were filled with tears and rage. "Why? *Why!*"

Siroth then saw Grull beside the dreamer, and he began to suspect that the apparition might be real after all.

"Guess who woke up," said Grull.

Siroth passed out again.

Grull took the arm of the seething dreamer, turning him away from the unconscious Prez. Blood still spattered the operating room, smeared into the wood with wet rags but not quite cleaned after the operation.

"Come along now. Let's have a chat." The blind man leaned heavily on the dreamer's arm, hoping to calm the other man. Grull guided him down a corridor where smoky torches had long ago replaced broken fluorescent lights.

"What's your name, dreamer? I am Grull."

The old torturer could not see the tears drying on the dreamer's cheeks, but he could feel the breath of the man's answer on his own face. "Aragon."

"How come you're still alive, Aragon, when none of your other companions woke up?"

"All our stations were monitored by delicate computer systems, with triple-nested backup functions. It's more of a surprise that no one else survived." Aragon took a deep breath, and Grull felt a faint shudder pass through the other's body. "My station was at the far end of the vault. Maybe your paranoid Prez had exhausted himself by then."

They said nothing more until they emerged into the open air from Siroth's great square castle that bore the crumbling words *First National Bank* across its facade. They walked through a courtyard and Aragon stopped short, but Grull pulled him over to a stone bench in the sun. The stunned dreamer didn't resist.

The *First National Bank* castle rested at the top of a gentle hill, just high enough that the view stretched out to engulf the ruins of a city below. Streets had turned into lawns; roofs and walls had collapsed. An accidental forest of fast-growing, genetically engineered trees had grown up alongside the buildings.

The blind man let Aragon stare speechless down at the dismal panorama for long moments. The dreamer finally managed to choke out a whisper, sounding betrayed. "How long has it been?"

"Sixty years." He sat down on the cold stone seat and patted it, motioning the dreamer to join him. "I was too young to remember much about those few hours of madness when *Before* turned to *After*. Somebody screaming 'Get To the Shelter Get To The Shelter!' Something exploded in front of my face, spectacular, searing white fire, sort of a grand finale to my eyesight.

"I was eight years old. For a little while I lived on whatever I could find. Then a religious cult, 'The Apocalypse Now,' found me and took me in. They believed they had been chosen to rebuild the world exactly as God intended it to be, to the death of all nonbelievers. And here I was, a blind child who had miraculously survived the holocaust. Perfect prophet material."

He shrugged a little to himself, and had no way of knowing whether Aragon was paying attention. "But I never turned out to be what they wanted. I was smart enough to know I'd never make it alone, so I played along with them. The Apocalypse Now treated me with respect—*they* all died by the age of thirty from cancer or genetic defect, but I just kept getting older.

"The fukkups were being born then, every one of them with the wrong number of arms, legs, even heads. Something about the war, biological weapons rearranging everyone's genes. Most of the mutants were so messed up they died anyway, or the mothers would throw them away, or kill them—but some survived. At first they must have hidden in the ruins or in the burned-out forest, horrified of themselves and the others of their kind. But then they started banding together, venting their anger at the normals. You know, terrorizing the countryside, mutilating people to look like themselves.

"Of course, I had a distorted view of it all, living in the Apocalypse Now. But there were plenty of other hunter groups, or communes, or scavengers, and they all came together for defense under a new leader, the Prez. Prez Mecas, Siroth's father, managed to unite his realm with a few other Prezes and with the Apocalypse Now. Together, they managed to cut the marauding fukkups to pieces. Now we keep them all in a huge corral where they can rot on their feet for all we care. Sero uses them for his experiments, or Siroth plays with them on hunting games now and then. They've been made pretty much harmless."

Aragon didn't seem to know which expression to keep on his face. He sat silent, stunned, as if looking desperately for some way to survive his despair.

"After the fukkups were brought under control, the Prezes took to fighting among themselves—assholes, none of them had any *real* concept of leadership. Any given Prez might last a year or two before he was assassinated. Prez Mecas was a lousy dictator—didn't know how to hold people in fear of him, never listened to anyone's counsel because he was too busy with his own pleasure. He didn't know how to be careful.

"I had become Master Torturer of the Apocalypse

Now. I went to his son Siroth because I knew I could train him to be a real Prez. We trapped Mecas in his chambers, tangling him in his own sheets, and fed him to the fukkups. Siroth didn't show any regret whatsoever. I knew he would make it, then. Love is one thing a Prez cannot have."

"A good leader should love his people above all else," Aragon muttered, but he seemed too stunned to begin an argument. "My God, the mess we left behind was the Golden Age of Mankind."

Grull frowned. "How can you possibly call *Before* a mess, compared to what we have now?"

"We still had plenty of problems. I kept finding perfect solutions to them—but people wouldn't *listen*. They said my solutions were 'wildly unrealistic' and that I should come down to the Real World. I never found their Real World—I found Draigen instead."

Grull detected bitterness in the dreamer's words, but they took a subtly different tone, as if Aragon were no longer speaking from his heart, but from a speech Draigen had given. He heard the dreamer stand up and shout toward the ruins at the bottom of the hill. "We understood things nobody else did. We could plan ahead. We could see the wisest things to say and do—but everyone was so bogged down with whether the books balanced, whether they would get the promotion, what kind of deodorant to use, what to cook for dinner . . . they never learned to understand life. We *understood* it!" He turned back to Grull, sitting motionless on the stone bench.

"I became an agricultural engineer, a damn good one, to solve the world's food shortage—and you know what? Nobody *wanted* me to! All the money spent to bring huge tractors, better seed and fertilizer to poor countries—and the minute we turn our backs the savages let our shining tractors sit there unused while they go back out in the fields with their oxen and scratch plows, because 'that was the way their forefathers grew the crops.' Nobody seemed to remember that their forefathers died of malnutrition. They *wanted* to starve!

How can a perfect solution work if people don't cooperate?"

"People, by nature, don't cooperate," Grull muttered.

"The seven of us under Draigen cooperated," Aragon said defensively. "All lonely revolutionaries, totally devoted to saving the world . . . but the world wasn't ready for us. Draigen had his dream. We were to make the world pure and good and right for all mankind. Why didn't anyone else want it that way? How can I carry on that great vision by *myself*?" he moaned.

Grull directed his sightless eyes into the breeze. "Now do you understand why Prez Siroth could never let your group wake up?"

Aragon shuddered, as if suddenly remembering who Grull was. The old man let the dreamer sit in an uninterrupted, awkward silence, waiting for him to deal with his churning emotions. Aragon surprised the blind old man by sighing in apparent defeat.

"Your Prez had taken Draigen's heart. And now you're going to take his eyes. Isn't that enough?"

Grull found himself thinking back to the dim childhood memories he normally kept tightly locked away, answering a different question. "My mother had a large flower garden filled with roses and snapdragons. My father took me to the big city once . . . I can still feel how *tall* those shining buildings were." He fell silent for a moment, then, "Yes, I would like to see again. But I doubt that Doctor Sero is capable of performing the transplant."

Aragon looked at him, raising his eyebrows. "Surely if this surgeon can transplant a heart, he can give you new eyes?"

"Siroth is a quick-healer. Sero could probably have *dropped* the heart into his chest and he would have survived. I am just a blind old man."

The dreamer smiled, and Grull could smell a strange excitement in Aragon's body scent. "Vesalius, the surgeon with our group, could have performed the operation easily. Too bad your Prez killed him. But we still have our medical knowledge in the vault, in a place